Carol Lefevre holds a Ph.D. in Creative Writing from the University of Adelaide, where she is a Visiting Research Fellow. Her two previous novels are *If You Were Mine* (2008) and *Nights in the Asylum* (2007), which was shortlisted for the Commonwealth Writers' Prize and won the Nita B. Kibble Award. Her non-fiction book *Quiet City: Walking in West Terrace Cemetery* (2016) was shortlisted for the South Australian Festival Awards for Literature. In 2017 she was Writer-in-Residence at the J.M. Coetzee Centre for Creative Practice. Carol lives in Adelaide.

The
HAPPINESS
Glass

Carol Lefevre

First published by Spinifex Press, Australia, 2018

Spinifex Press Pty Ltd
PO Box 5270, North Geelong, Victoria 3215
PO Box 105, Mission Beach, Queensland 4852
Australia

women@spinifexpress.com.au
www.spinifexpress.com.au

Editors: Susan Hawthorne and Pauline Hopkins
Cover photograph by Beverley Hiscock
Author photograph by Chris Lefevre
Internal photographs: "Argent Street, c1957"
by Sheila Hiscock; all others by the author.
Cover design by Deb Snibson, MAPG
Typeset in Australia by Helen Christie
Designed and typeset in Adobe Garamond Pro
Printed by McPherson's Printing Group

Australian Government

A catalogue record for this book is available from the National Library of Australia

9781925581638 (paperback)
9781925581645 (ebook : pdf)
9781925581669 (ebook : epub)
9781925581652 (ebook : Kindle)

Australia Council for the Arts

This project has been assisted by the Australian Government through the Australia Council, its principal arts funding and advisory body.

MIX
Paper from responsible sources
FSC
www.fsc.org FSC® C001695

In memory of my father
Peter Ernest Hiscock
(1923–1972)

'Fire that's closest kept burns most of all.'
William Shakespeare

Contents

ONE

Burning with Madame Bovary

1.

> The street – the only one – is about a gunshot in
> length, has a few shops on either side, and stops
> short at the end of the road.
>
> *Madame Bovary,* Flaubert

In the furnace heat of late summer, 1956, I started school in
Wilcannia. It was the year the British government began its
bomb tests at Maralinga, and Amy Witting's first published
short story 'The Strait of Hellespont' appeared in *Southerly*.
There is no photograph of my milestone morning, and none of
the schoolhouse – a small, dust-plain building in which seven
grades sat facing the front in its single, stifling, unadorned
classroom. My mother owned a box Brownie camera, but she
might not have had a roll of film for it that day, or the money
to buy one. Then again, photographs were often ruined when
handling those early cameras: if the back was inadvertently
opened, a burst of Outback light was all it took to burn-out an
image. And even if a photograph was taken, our family moved

many times in the years that followed: inevitably, things were lost; they were left behind, or discarded.

In place of a photograph there are flashes of memory: children standing in ragged lines on the unpaved playground; pepper trees in dusty corners of the yard; a huddle of white mothers, talking and laughing; a few black mothers who had risen early to cross the iron bridge over the Darling River, small children shyly clinging to their cotton skirts. I must have been excited to be starting school, a child who was already a fluent reader. Perhaps it was the line-up that rattled my confidence, a sense of the beginning of submissiveness. At the last moment I refused to join the other children, and when the teacher insisted, I kicked her in the shins and bolted.

My mother still remembers the uproar but has forgotten the double-decker wooden pencil case she offered as a bribe. It was the most desirable object in the town. I must have seen it in a shop and been told it was too expensive, but my poor mother, who detests a fuss, promised that I should have it if I would stand in line. So I swallowed my tears, and the hastily acquired pencil case was in my hands before lunch. Its sliding lid fitted smoothly; its two sections swivelled to reveal the secret lower chamber; pencils sat snugly inside, with a small compartment for an eraser and a sharpener. I would line up again today for such a treasure.

A frontier town in north-west New South Wales, Wilcannia's name is said to derive from an Aboriginal word that means 'gap in the bank where floodwaters escape', or else it means 'wild dog', or it means neither of these things. Back in the 1880s it was an important river port, with thirteen hotels and its own newspaper, the *Western Grazier,* started by an Irish printer and journalist, James Smith Reid. By the time we came to live in Wilcannia its glory days were over, but the Knox &

Downs store, where you could buy almost anything, was still in business, and the nineteenth-century sandstone buildings that had sprung up in the town's heyday were not yet derelict or boarded up, as they would be twenty years later.

One of the first Europeans to explore the area in 1835 was Major Thomas Mitchell, poet, painter, and the last man in Australia to fight a duel. At one time two of Charles Dickens's sons, and one of Anthony Trollope's, were listed as members of the Wilcannia Cricket Club. Remote and inhospitable as a star, Wilcannia had a certain swagger.

Our rented house on Reid Street backed on to the Darling River. There were struggling fruit trees and a dilapidated hen house in the long backyard, which fell away to the tea-coloured, slow-flowing river. The water was said to be treacherous, mined with potholes and fallen branches, and with sly currents that would tug you from the bank and suck you under. But in those endless, battering summers, warnings often went unheeded, and a child drowned in the river the year I started school – a small white boy, burdened with a clumpy boot and leg brace from his brush with childhood polio.

The snaking river divided white from black, with the iron, centre-lift bridge between, but at school I shared a desk with an Aboriginal girl called Anna. Her people would have been Barkindji, which I now know means 'belonging to the river'. After school I walked home to the house on Reid Street, while Anna crossed the bridge to the makeshift shelters we could see from the bottom of our yard. Whole families lived there in the semi-open without even basic facilities, and at night, especially, we could hear them – laughing, singing, quarrelling – and smell the smoke from their campfires.

The separation of black and white in 1950s Australia is a thread in Amy Witting's 'The Strait of Hellespont', a story in which party guests discuss a row that has raged in the newspapers over whether Aborigines should be allowed to use the local baths. When challenged on her opinion that the letter writers don't know what they're talking about, one of the characters, Morna Christie, spits out that the blacks are "riddled with disease". Morna is temporarily silenced by Iris Lunney, who points out that a white man with the pox can still use the baths: "the dirty word exploded from her mouth like a little firecracker of anger". But Morna is not crushed; if anything, her view hardens.

I have often tried to put myself back into that Wilcannia classroom, curious to know how and what we were taught, and how we children got along together. But all I can glean from memory are a few trivial facts: we were given slates and chalk to write our first letters; in the airless afternoons it was impossible not to fall asleep; most of us had bobbed hair, for there were no hairdressers, or if there were they were not for children.

On Reid Street, our next door neighbours were a white couple given to violent, alcohol-fuelled domestic arguments. The woman sometimes spoke to my mother over the fence, blaming her slurred speech on radiation from the tests at Maralinga. That year, four nuclear devices were exploded, code-named 'One Tree', 'Marcoo', 'Breakaway', and 'Kite'; the latter, released by a Royal Air Force bomber from a height of 35,000 feet, was the first British nuclear weapon to be dropped from an aircraft. The radioactive cloud from 'One Tree' reached a height of 37,500 feet, and radioactivity was recorded in South Australia, the Northern Territory, New South Wales, and Queensland.

Years later, at parties, when my mother had had a glass of wine or a beer, she would relate these conversations as amusing anecdotes.

"It's rrrrr…adiation!" She would roll the 'r' as our neighbour used to, roll her eyes, too, and flutter her eyelids, to general merriment.

It seems unthinkable that radioactive contamination could have raised a laugh, but the Maralinga tests were surrounded by such secrecy that for at least two decades people like my parents and their friends remained ignorant of the hazards. More puzzling is how our apparently alcohol-addled neighbour had acquired her grip on current affairs in a place where the outside world felt, and was, so far away. Perhaps in her hot little kitchen, nursing her bumps and bruises and her hangovers, she listened to the radio, although contemporary media coverage of the tests was tightly controlled, and weak. Chances are the couple had a son, or other relative, one of the Australian airmen who flew through the mushroom cloud, or one of the mechanics, builders, engineers, or servicemen – around eight-thousand of them – who were on the ground at Maralinga.

As for us, we had books, transported a box at a time from Broken Hill, or gathered by my father on long distance truck trips. We always had our noses in a book, and my precocious reading habit was formed in Wilcannia, for there really was nothing else to do, most evenings. Except sometimes in summer, when the supply of books dried up, or the heat inside the house became unbearable, then we would lie outside on a blanket, telling stories and stargazing.

2.

In the back-yard you could hear the chickens
squawking as the servant girl chased after them to
wring their necks.

Madame Bovary, Flaubert

After a succession of primary schools, five in all, I started high
school in Mount Gambier. All was going smoothly until the
curriculum for girls was split: one stream of students would
study French, Latin, English, and art, while the others would
take typing, and shorthand, and bookkeeping, the so-called
Commercial Course. I forget what the first choice was called,
but it was the one I wanted. However, my father put his foot
down firmly on this silliness: I would learn shorthand and
typing so that I could earn a living; it was up to him to ensure
I would never starve. I wept for a week, and my arguments
for French and Latin and art were ignored. Back then, fathers
made those choices, and daughters mostly obeyed.

I was inconsolable, although looking back I cannot blame
my father. He was from a working class family – miners, farm
workers, jacks of all trades – and had done his apprenticeship
as a fitter and turner in Broken Hill. As the eldest of four
children raised during the depression years, he knew how hard
it could be to put food on the table. He had hated his trade
and left the mines as soon as he could, and in an astonishing
career leap that I'm not sure would happen today he went from
driving trucks loaded with wool or goats around the Outback,
to working in radio, and later in television. But he knew that
lucky breaks were rare, and he had resolved that I would be
equipped to support myself.

If bookkeeping was dull, shorthand was at least a kind of language. But the typing class was a form of brainwashing in which we sat with our hands under the typewriter covers and chanted in unison: a s d f ; l k j, *ad infinitum*. These were the home keys on the heavy machines on which we were taught to type until our wrists and fingers ached – Imperial, Olivetti, Remington. Girls often fainted in typing class, slipping off hard, upright chairs and under the desks, overwhelmed by the noise, the numbing boredom, and what Isobel Callaghan in Amy Witting's *I for Isobel* calls the "misery" of "dehumanising solitude". Meanwhile, other girls, the girls I envied, were studying French. Somehow I acquired the text book and tried to teach myself in private, weeping over words I was uncertain how to pronounce. They were as mysterious and lovely as the elements of a spell, those words. The French language itself was a spell, I felt certain, if only I could learn to cast it.

But what did teenage girls in country towns want with Latin and French and art? What use would it be to them? I see now that the girls I envied were allowed to choose those subjects because their parents knew it would make no difference: when they left school they would marry and have children; they would stay at home and keep house. So where once I was furious that my father's vision for my future was so small, so stunted, with hindsight I realise that – by his lights, and at that time – it had actually been quite grand.

3.

And all the time, deep within her, she was waiting
for something to happen. Like a shipwrecked sailor
she scanned her solitude with desperate eyes for the
sight of a white sail far off on the misty horizon.
She had no idea what that chance would be...

Madame Bovary, Flaubert

Emma Bovary's craving for an indefinable excitement, her
longing for colour, must have been commonplace among
young women in these years I am writing about. The cultural
explosion in the 1960s was slow to shake South Australia, and
girls like me, unwilling to accept life as it had been laid out
for them – its ordinariness, its drudgery – and for whom a
university education seemed unreachable, were forced to live
much of the time in a dream world. It was a craving like Emma
Bovary's that plunged me into, and out of, an early marriage.
It sent me flying across the Tasman, alone for the first time in
my life, and sustained only by those modest skills acquired in
typing class. As it turned out, I was grateful for them.

The wooden houses of Wellington were quaint; its hills
were lush, its bays sparkling. I found employment as a typist in
the newsroom at the New Zealand Broadcasting Corporation.
Then, three months after I had arrived, my father died.
I returned to Sydney for his funeral, and in the disorienting
days of grief there I was sorely tempted to pick up the threads
of my old life and stay. And yet I returned to Wellington.
In letters home I had complained of its dowdiness, and its
freezing winter, but the city, and the small place in it that I had
begun to make for myself, was like a dream that I wanted to
keep on dreaming.

After a few false starts I found myself living in a yellow wooden house on Tinakori Road in Thorndon. It was Katherine Mansfield territory, and the settings of her short stories were all around. The rent was twenty-five dollars a week; it was a stretch on my typist's salary, but I loved the house fiercely. It was where I began to write, though I never dared whisper, even to myself, that I might become a writer. At work, surrounded by young, university-educated journalists, I was ashamed of having cut short my schooling. In conversation I skated over that fact as best I could, for I could not help equating a lack of education with stupidity. But a spark was struck there in the house in Thorndon; who knows why or how. On Friday afternoons I would borrow a typewriter from work, and struggle up the long hill of Bowen Street with it in my arms.

My flat was on the top floor – one bedroom, bathroom, a kitchen and sitting room with windows overlooking the Wellington Botanic Garden – and my front door, mine alone, was at the back, approached via a little curved footbridge: it was a house from fairy tale.

The kitchen had a gas stove and an ancient fridge, but no pots and pans. After moving in, I walked down Tinakori Road to the dairy to buy something for tea, and the soft-faced Maori woman behind the counter greeted me with a sunny smile.

"No pans! Hey, don't worry, I got plenty." Beaming, she pressed a frying pan and a battered aluminium saucepan into my hands. "Bring them back when you're ready," she said.

I carried home baked beans, bread, and a tin opener, but it was only with her saucepan on the stove that I realised the gas was disconnected. I ate the beans cold, and mixed Milo with hot water from the shower. That night I froze under a single thin blanket, and finally rose at three, shivering, to spread clothes from my suitcase over the bed.

I lived in that house as girls of slender means have lived in flats and bedsits all over the world, and in stories, relishing my independence one minute and wringing my hands over my impoverished circumstances the next. Others recognised the fairy tale of a girl living alone in a little wooden house on a hill, and they found their way over the footbridge: once, late at night, a television journalist I knew slightly arrived without shoes, having fled her violent husband. I made up a bed for her on the sofa, but that is another story – or perhaps it does belong here in this account of how it was sometimes, to be young and female in the second half of the twentieth century.

Despite the occasional visitors, I spent much time alone in the buttercup house, including the loneliest few days of my life. It was the New Year's Eve after my father died – the night before my twenty-second birthday; I sat at the kitchen window watching tail lights diminish up Tinakori hill, and celebrated at midnight with raspberries and cream, and a glass of wine from the bottle the landlord had left for Christmas. I didn't see anyone to speak to until the third of January, when I returned to work. In a letter to my mother I wrote: *I'm getting too old to attach much importance to birthdays, but it would be nice to have a happy one. I haven't enjoyed a birthday since I was small and used to get a party dress, and an ice-cream cake, and a doll.* It was the closest I ever came to Isobel Callaghan's uncelebrated birthday, though Amy Witting would not finish writing *I for Isobel* until 1979, and the book would not fall into my hands until the century had turned.

In Thorndon I started French lessons; I beat out letters on the borrowed typewriter, and tentatively began a children's novel. When the family who lived downstairs said they could hear me typing I told them I was studying, and since I always stopped at a reasonable hour they remained good-natured.

In Amy Witting's story 'The Writing Desk', young, aspiring writer Emily pretends to her dreadful landlady that she is writing a thesis rather than admit she is working on a novel. Witting's young women, like Emily, and Isobel Callaghan, know that there is something about a girl reading, writing, and showing a preference for solitude that provokes people. According to Isobel it contravenes The Eleventh Commandment: *Thou shalt not be different.* As well as these first fumbling attempts at writing I still had my nose in a book, and at weekends I would read all night because there was no one to say I couldn't. But after a year I had to relinquish the buttercup house; its beauty was a luxury I had never really been able to afford. Even the landlord shed a tear for me, though he did not offer to lower the rent.

In *The Poetics of Space*, French philosopher Gaston Bachelard says of the houses we have lived in: "All our lives we come back to them in our daydreams." When researching our old address in Wilcannia on the Internet, I was strangely stirred by photographs of houses in the town. I did not know them, but felt a throb of recognition, and sorrow for their bleakness. There it is, I thought, the foundation of melancholy laid down by ill-shaped rooms with concrete floors, by utilitarian windows, and the desolation they framed – landscapes as parched as the mournful cry of a crow – a dark layer of longing concealed at the bottom of every bleach-bright day.

As a child, of course, the Reid Street house was simply where we lived, it was home, and it is only my fortunate present that allows me to look back and judge it harshly. But my thoughts return often to the buttercup house where, despite the loneliness, and surviving much of the time on toast and tea, the dream still brings only a buzz of joy. Yet it is only one of many houses that have sheltered me, and they are all inside me still; I remember the patterns of their wallpapers, I could reach out in the dark and find their doorknobs and their light switches.

4.

> So Paris swam before her eyes, like a shifting ocean,
> glimmering through a rose-coloured haze.
>
> *Madame Bovary*, Flaubert

In a second-hand shop on Tinakori Road, I bought a set of the short stories of Guy de Maupassant, nine volumes, hardbound. When I left Wellington for South Africa, and eventually London, I carried them in my luggage, and I cannot begin to list the occasions when their presence there caused complications, let alone explain why I clung to them so tenaciously.

The South African adventure was a dangerous folly. I went with a friend, a journalist, who had read Trevor Huddleston's *Naught for Your Comfort* and decided on a whim to have a look at the place. Television had just started up there, and a sound operator we knew had written to say that there was plenty of work. However, by the time we pitched up for interviews it had all become a lot more difficult. Broadcasting in apartheid-era South Africa was government-run and tightly controlled, and its employees were required to be bi-lingual – English and Afrikaans. With a shortage of trained sound operators, they had fudged the rules for our friend, but a foreign journalist was regarded with suspicion. By association, I had no chance.

We were thrown into a labour market where the jobs traditionally undertaken by travellers were filled by black or coloured people. For other work, our visas revealed that we would not be long-term employees. Starvation was suddenly a very real prospect, until a chance encounter yielded news of a vacancy for two live-in barmaids at a hotel up the coast. The deal was done by telephone, to our great relief, and we took the train to Mossel Bay, where the Hotel Santos faced, across a dusty road and a narrow railway line, the perfect blue expanse of the Indian Ocean. Sun-faded, and flanked by palms, it looked like the setting for a Somerset Maugham story.

The first shock was that we were to appear before a magistrate, who would decide whether we were of sufficiently moral character to be barmaids. Since we had only just stepped off the train, and there was no one to vouch for our characters, moral or otherwise, Gerry the Dutch hotel manager went with us to the interview, and undertook to guarantee our behaviour. The second shock was that news of our imminent appearance in the Hotel's Ladies' Bar had spread, and on our first evening shift – the first behind a bar for either of us – the room was packed with rugged men with ruddy sun-damaged faces. Their silent scrutiny unnerved us, to say the least, and not know-ing the names of the drinks, or how to pour them, was, by comparison, a minor embarrassment.

Liquored-up, the men began to speak in Afrikaans. The manager appeared then and threatened to close the bar. They were to speak English in front of us, he said, and treat us with respect. He was such an unlikely knight, but knight he surely was. Afterwards, he explained that the men had been discussing us in coarse language, and although we had not understood what they said, he apologised on their behalf.

The first-floor bar, with its bay windows facing the sea and a view of the Outeniqua Mountains, was a pleasant enough place to work, but the space behind the bar was strangely set up, with a screened-off area that seemed to serve no purpose.

This turned out to be where, until very recently, drinks had been prepared: since the business of pouring alcohol into a glass might somehow corrupt the women whose husbands brought them to the Ladies' Bar on Saturday nights, bottles had been kept out of sight, and the barman would slip out the back to mix the drinks. We had noticed that the women who came into the bar never made eye contact with us. When we approached to ask what they would like to drink, they would turn and whisper to their husbands, and the husbands would relay their order. At first, we thought this was hilarious, but as time went on it grated.

Our room was in an annexe close to the hotel kitchen; it had a concrete floor and a few pieces of plain furniture. With working alternate lunchtime shifts, every second day was free for one of us until six in the evening, and on those long, hot, empty afternoons I would read, or walk along the dusty road to the town's public library. I carried back framed prints for our empty walls – Van Gogh's *Café Terrace at Night* was renewed again and again.

In a letter to his sister Wilhelmina about that picture, Vincent asked whether she had yet read Guy de Maupassant's *Bel-Ami*, and what she thought of the writer's talent. The beginning of *Bel-Ami* described a starry night in Paris, with lighted cafés shining along the dark boulevards. It was very like the subject Vincent was painting, and in asking his sister's opinion of de Maupassant's talent he was, indirectly, asking about his own.

In that hot little room on the east coast of Africa, with Vincent's lighted café at the foot of my bed, I vanished into Alexandre Dumas' novels – *The Three Musketeers, Twenty Years After, The Vicomte de Bragelonne, Louise de la Valliere, The Man in the Iron Mask* – those swashbuckling tales, with their intricate plotlines. I revelled in Zola's macabre *Thérèse Raquin*. I read Balzac, and, for the first time, Flaubert's masterpiece, closing my book each evening only to go to the bar where, like a somnambulist, I went through the motions of serving drinks to customers who would become so many 'Yonville peasants'.

5.

What will become of me? What help can I hope
for? What consolation? What relief?

Madame Bovary, Flaubert

As a young woman, my mother longed to go to art school. At the School of Arts and Crafts in Adelaide she could have been taught by Mary P. Harris and Dorrit Black, but instead she was sent to learn shorthand and typing. In patriarchal post-war Australia, millions of letters were dictated – invariably by men – and dispatched – invariably to other men – via the well-drilled, helpless hands of innumerable young women. When the responses came, women filed them. To dodge this fate required greater reserves of courage and money than either I or my mother possessed. In Amy Witting's *I For Isobel*, when Trevor, one of the university students Isobel Callaghan has befriended, asks why she doesn't go to university, Isobel says, "I have to earn a living." Trevor responds that it is "rotten luck", but to Isobel, the money she earns and her ability to earn it are fundamental to her precarious independence.

Aside from the typing, I was barely educated; as time went on I would resort more and more to self-teaching, and it would be decades before I set foot inside a university. My mother would wait forty years until both her father and my father had died, to enrol at art school at the age of sixty. She gained her diploma, but it was, she said wistfully, too late for her to do anything with it.

For Emma Bovary there was no possibility of work outside the home. Emma seeks to escape the drudgery of farm life in marriage, but marriage does not bring control of her own destiny. Burning for something she can barely name, she plunges into a clandestine affair, and then another. Her character does eventually become ugly, distorted by extravagance, desire, and – worse even than adultery – indifference to her daughter. Yet from one so tightly held, from a wife and mother who is still a child herself, from a woman denied expression, except through her domestic role, surely ugly behaviour might be expected.

An academic friend who has taught *Madame Bovary* tells me that, without exception, her students hated Emma. Young female undergraduates – beneficiaries of the struggles of suffragettes and feminists in the century before they were born – can afford to despise her weakness. But as Emma's extravagance casts her deeper and deeper into debt, men offer help in return for sexual favours; even her suicide is only possible because the chemist's assistant is attracted to her. After her death, others act despicably: the piano teacher sends an account for three months' lessons, though Emma never had even one; Félicité, Emma's servant, takes to wearing Madame's dresses, and eventually flits from the town with the remains of her mistress's wardrobe; Homais the chemist discourages his children from intimacy with little Berthe Bovary, in view of the difference in their social position. No one emerges from this story with honour.

In the end, all that is left to Madame Bovary is death, and when Charles looks upon his wife's corpse it comes as a relief to the reader to realise that she is free at last.

"On Emma's satin dress, white as a moonbeam, the watering shimmered. She disappeared beneath it. It seemed to him as if she were escaping from herself and melting confusedly into everything about her, into the silence, the night, the passing wind, the damp odours rising."

As with life, fiction is filled with Emma Bovary characters. Lily Knight McClellan in Joan Didion's *Run River*, published in the same year as Betty Friedan's *The Feminine Mystique*, is a product of the myth that a woman will only find true fulfilment in matrimony. Like Emma, Lily McClellan looks outside her marriage, and though the consequences are bloody, Lily survives, scented with *Joy* by Jean Patou. Nora Porteous in Jessica Anderson's *Tirra Lirra by the River* is a version of Emma. On the verge of splitting with her odious husband, Nora is filled with panic, "and a longing for the undemanding dullness and steady misery of my captivity."

Isobel Callaghan's landlady, Mrs Bowers, expresses the social mood still prevalent in my girlhood when she says, "I always say, if a girl has a decent engagement ring, she has something of her own", and modern young women might be amazed to learn that plenty of people would have agreed with her. Isobel appears for the last time in the short story 'Soft Toys' published in *Faces and Voices* (2000). Amy Witting died while in the early stages of writing her third Isobel novel, and the Isobel of 'Soft Toys' – single, pregnant, and planning to live in an uninsulated wash-house once her baby is born – offers a clue to the next phase of her life. We will never know how she might have managed in these circumstances, and those of us who have loved Isobel Callaghan will be forever anxious about her – she plans to keep on writing, but the odds are against it.

When questioned about the identity of Emma Bovary, Flaubert famously declared "Madame Bovary, *c'est moi!*" Casting back over my own life, especially the parts of it revisited here, I exclaim with Flaubert: "*C'est moi! Je suis Emma!*" For although in the end I did go to university I never conquered French or Latin – it was too late for that dream. Like Isobel Callaghan, I did eventually accept that I could become a writer, but life still teems with Madame Bovary moments, and this is the truth at the heart of Flaubert's great novel, the reason it has endured: we are all, in our own ways, Madame Bovary.

In Emma's drawn-out downfall we recognise our own dark struggles, the desert of days in which we measure longing against need and calculate the inevitable shortfall. Alongside dreams we strive to wake from, and those we strive to keep on dreaming, there is, too, the shadowing darkness of history.

Looking back, I see that we never belonged in Wilcannia, and that the Barkindji, who *did* belong, had long since had their peace and their way of life destroyed. For in his quest to explore along the Darling River, Major Thomas Livingston Mitchell, poet, painter, failed duellist, was responsible for the deaths of seven Aboriginal people near Mount Dispersion, and an unknown number between Menindee and Wilcannia. He was also responsible, in the vicinity of Lake Repose, for the separation of a very young Aboriginal child from her mother. The girl, Ballandella, returned with Mitchell to Sydney, where although she was introduced into his family with a degree of affection she was really a kind of living exhibit from Mitchell's expedition.

In one of those drifts of direction language often takes, the Anglo-Saxon word 'wyrd' once meant fate or destiny before its modern meaning of odd, or strange. An assessment of one's wyrd, or fate, must begin with where and when one was born. After that it depends on what you think and do, and who you meet. For the relative safety and privilege of post-war rural

Australia, where my greatest trial was being made to master the typewriter, I count myself fortunate. The impulse that drives a writer is as instinctive as that of a sea turtle hatchling that digs itself from the sand and scuttles towards the ocean, and touch typing has been useful to me in a way my father could never have foreseen. Like turtle hatchlings, writers are rarely blessed with ideal conditions. I started school in Wilcannia, but I have seen Paris. Most days, that is enough.

The Stars of the Milky Way

Beth and I are balanced on perches inside the chook house, crouching comfortably, with our elbows bent and flapping like wings. It is an ordinary Wilcannia afternoon – hot and flat as the bottom of an iron – with nothing more interesting to offer than teasing the hens. The weight of the sky presses the air out of town in summer. You can see it in photographs, people looking as if it is almost too much effort to breathe. The divorce and death rates soar in the hot months. No one gives us kids details, of course: people simply disappear, amid whispers, and knowing looks, and a fine red dust collecting on the surface of things.

Beyond our back fence the Darling River sidles, olive green and shallow in this droughty year. From inside the house comes the bleat of the wireless. Mum is in there trying to ignore the heat as she damps down laundry, sprinkling cotton pillowcases with rainwater from her old tomato sauce bottle with holes punched in the lid, rolling them into sausages for ironing. She has been cranky all day because of the ruckus last night.

Yesterday evening, while she was out watering, our neighbour, Dorrie Brickle, appeared at the gap in the fence and said something in that stuck-up voice Mum swears is the fakest thing she has ever heard.

"It's rr…radiation damage, Missus Brennan."

Dorrie has strange pale eyes – sheep's eyes, our father calls them – and a skin that flares into a rash at the least excitement. With her black fluffy hair tucked out of sight under a scarf, her thin little face, with nothing to soften it, looked both too intense and exceptionally plain.

"Causes sterility in both sexes," she said.

Mum's fingers tightened around the hose, and she shot an anxious look to where we stood fiddling with Beth's old pedal car.

"It's wrecked my memory," Dorrie continued. "In rr… repertory my lines were perfect. Whole scripts. I prided myself. But since these bomb tests, I can hardly remember what happened yesterday."

Our mother aimed a stream of water into the trough surrounding the base of a young peach tree and muttered something neutral. She has her own theories about Dorrie Brickle's memory lapses.

Later, we were lying on our backs on the tiny square of front lawn, scouring the night sky for a sight of Sputnik; cricket song, the throbbing soundtrack to summer, was broken by occasional bursts of music from across the river.

Beth said, "How many stars are there in the Milky Way?" She is always hunting facts. "Roughly."

Just as she said it, shouts and crashes erupted next door.

"Countless," said Mum, her voice calm as she leaned towards the slamming of the Brickles' back door.

"But there must be a number."

"Yes, but no one knows for sure," Mum said, "so whatever we say can never be exact."

"But–"

"Dorrie, let me in!" Mr Brickle attacked the door with his knuckles.

From inside their house came the tinkle of breaking glass.

"Lily, take your sister indoors and make a jug of raspberry cordial." Mum's old cane chair creaked.

"I don't want any cordial," Beth said. Sometimes she can be incredibly dense, or else much more cunning than we give her credit for.

"Never mind!" Mum jumped up and jabbed a finger at the house.

We dawdled towards the front door, which stands wide open on breathless nights, our ears straining towards Brickles' place.

"If you don't open this door right now–"

Beth and I stared at each other wide-eyed, imagining the consequences for Dorrie Brickle, but as it turned out, we were wrong. Our neighbours' back door opened; there was a thump, a shattering, followed by a rising wail and the solid slam of the door. Then Mr Brickle appeared, pressing his face to the gap in the fence and calling weakly for our mother.

Her sudden intake of breath carried across the yard.

"Mrs Brennan. Ginny! Help me. Help!" He was working up the kind of bawling tone young calves use to call their mothers.

"Just let me get my shoes on." Mum ran for the blanket on the lawn where she had kicked them off after tea.

Beth and I edged nearer, and in the light from their kitchen window we saw Mr Brickle's balding head where a dark patch oozed blood. It streamed on either side of his face in messy black lines, crazy paving set in the yellow kitchen light.

"I'm coming." Mum's voice was high and cheery and un-familiar. But by the time she reached the fence he had stumbled away, swallowed up by the darkness at the side of his house. "Oh Lord!" she muttered. "She must've hit him with a bottle."

From inside came further crashes, plates and glasses connecting with something solid.

"Listen, girls," Mum drew us back to the blanket on the lawn. "I want you to lie still for five minutes while I run to the phone box."

Beth began to grizzle, but Mum guided her firmly to the blanket.

"You can count the stars in the Milky Way," she said. "I expect you to be up to at least a hundred by the time I get back. Lily will help."

"But you said the stars were countless."

"Because no one has counted them yet," Mum said. "You can be the first." She took Beth's stubby forefinger and pointed it at the sky, jabbing with each number. "One, two, three, four, five."

"Six, seven, eight, nine, ten," continued Beth, calmed now by the wondrous light-rash above our heads. Mum gave my shoulder a nudge.

"Ten, eleven, twelve," I counted, falling into Beth's rhythm.

Mum paused for a moment on the edge of the blanket, listening. From beyond the fence came a splintering sound, and at that she turned and galloped away towards the front gate.

We had reached one-hundred-and-fifty-seven by the time Mr Brickle broke through his own back door. Between counting stars we followed the progress of the battle from room to room, the blows, grunts, shrieks, and curses, only faintly muffled by the flimsy walls of their house.

"Who do you think is winning?" whispered Beth.

"I don't know."

A moment of quiet was cracked by a gunshot; it seemed to ricochet off the Brickles' tin roof and into space, silencing the crickets. Beth's hand groped for mine on the blanket, but she kept her eyes fixed steadily on the sky.

"One-hundred-and-eighty-one," she said after a bit, "one-hundred-and-eighty-two."

Lunchtime, the police are still at the Brickles' house. Mr Brickle was driven off in the back of the police wagon last night, but we haven't seen or heard anything of Dorrie. Beth and I watch silently from the lawn as the police carry out something covered with a green blanket and then, with nothing happening, drift away down the yard and perch in the stuffy gloom of the chook house. It is not the mindless antics of the hens that draws us but the lure of a wasps' nest high up in a dark back corner. We dare each other to poke it with a stick and have to run for our lives when the wasps turn nasty.

Our mother gets out the calamine lotion, and Beth, peering with interest at my stung shoulder, says, "There are one-hundred-and-ninety-seven stars in the Milky Way."

Mum stoops over us, her eyes anxious as she scans Beth's freckled and slightly sunburnt face; her fingertips are white where she grips the bottle.

"It was hard," Beth says, "with all the noise. But Lily and I counted a-hundred-and-ninety-seven stars," she says. "So now they're not countless."

Mum saturates a cotton ball with calamine and dabs at the place where the wasp's sting has left a puncture mark.

"One-hundred-and-ninety-seven?" she says.

"Yep!" Beth looks smug.

"Well thank the Lord for one less mystery to be solved," Mum says, and when she's finished with the calamine she gathers us, one under each arm. "Let's wash your faces and we'll walk to Murphy's for an ice cream." Her palms slide over our shoulders until she's cupping a chin in each of her hands.

"Goody! I want pink ice cream," Beth shrieks.

Mum squats on the yellow lino to rub a flannel over her grubby fingers.

We never go to Murphy's unless we've got birthday money, or it's near Christmas. Mum picks up her old red purse, and as my mouth opens to ask her why we're having a treat she nudges me towards the front room.

"Lily, run and find your shoes," she says.

At the thought of pink ice cream, my mouth begins to water. Everything else goes right out of my head, as I rush to buckle on my sandals.

At the Hotel Santos

Josie van de Berg's first task each morning was to administer to Albert the cook a pill that would make him crawl on the ground like a snake at the first drop of alcohol. Albert was a good chef but he could not stay sober, and after mulling over the difficulties of replacing him, she and her husband had concluded that another might be just as bad.

"Better the devil you know," Gerry said.

Their doctor made up the pills to his own recipe. Albert swallowed one every morning while Josie watched it go down; he did not take the pill on his day off, and she paid extra for his enforced sobriety. At first Albert had been cocky, and sceptical about the pill, and the kitchen staff rolled their eyes when telling of the time he indulged himself with the cooking wine. Albert had writhed on the kitchen floor, as the Missus had promised, and now his mute despair as Josie produced the pill on her square, uncompromising palm each morning, was proof that he believed in its power.

Josie was a natural blonde, with a deep bosom, strong bones, large teeth and a big voice. Her ambition when young had been to sing like Shirley Bassey. Instead, she had married

Gerry and borne three blonde-haired children, and at almost forty, she seemed as calm and settled as her volcanic personality would ever allow. In summer, when the hotel was full, there was plenty to do in the kitchen, the linen room, and the Ladies' Bar. In winter, she took the train to Cape Town and visited her parents, a retired English couple, who were always astonished at the turbulent daughter they had produced.

A week before their tenth summer season opened, Josie and Gerry invited friends to the hotel for dinner. Afterwards they adjourned to the Ladies' Bar, where the man, a lanky, sun-stained farmer, fell into a nostalgic mood.

"Sing for us, Josie," he pleaded.

He'd had a bit to drink over dinner, and was now knocking back Van der Hum and brandy. His wife, shapeless after decades of childbearing, had just confided to Josie that she envied her hourglass figure. It was heavier than it used to be, Josie said. Ah, but it still went in and out, the wife insisted, which was more than she had managed.

"Just one song," coaxed the farmer.

Gerry smiled at his wife; to hear her sing gave him pleasure. Josie strode to the upright piano and felt her way through a few firm chords. Then, her smoky voice launched into a song in which she grasped the notes and tamed them. Her friends flopped back in their chairs and raised their glasses, and she finished to a ripple of applause.

"*Lekker, lekker,*" cried the farmers standing at the bar, regulars who drove into town for their Saturday night fill of beer, bright lights and feminine company.

"Sing another one, Josie," cried her friends.

"*Asseblief! Asseblief!*"

Josie was in the mood now, and she sat for an hour at the piano, hands roaming the yellowed keys and her throaty voice soaring through song after song. At closing time, a wiry little man with a moustache and bright bow tie slithered over and handed her his card: *Morley Trotter, Theatrical Agent and Promoter.*

"At your service, Madame."

Josie beamed at him: she knew she sang well, so it was pointless to affect modesty.

Next morning Mr Trotter appeared in the Ladies' Bar, where Josie was slicing lemons. The fruit were as big as oranges, with a dizzying, high-pitched scent. With fingers still sticky with the juice, Josie took his order for a pink gin and listened while he offered compliments.

"Wasted talent is a crime," he ventured.

His bow tie was fuchsia pink this morning, and Josie noted that his hair was a touch too dark for his complexion. Perhaps his work kept him away from fresh air and sunlight.

"I could fix you up with several most prestigious venues." He rubbed his hands together. "Durban, Port Elizabeth, even a top club in Jo'burg."

Trotter mentioned one or two of the artists he represented. Josie leaned closer; they were names she had heard of. A bronze flash like an eel stirring sediment in a stream flickered in her green eyes, as she absent-mindedly rubbed a little of the pungent lemon juice over the soft insides of her wrists.

During the long siesta, when guests retired to avoid the white afternoon light, Josie pulled on a bathing suit and crossed the road to the beach. She swam to the nearest of the three black barges anchored in the bay, and hauled herself up onto its rough, sun-bleached surface. There, with her head thrown back against the cobalt sky, she ran through her scales and vocal exercises. They were not bad, after all this time. Not bad at all. Back at the annexe flat she plunged her arms into her wardrobe and extracted dresses she hadn't worn in years. With her skin covered in a fine glitter of sea salt, she stepped into one, but the zip could not be closed.

Next morning, Josie ordered Albert to prepare a thin vegetable broth. She ate a bowl of it three times a day for a week, lost six pounds, and let an inch into the waistlines of her dresses. When a telegram arrived, she announced to her bewildered family that she was taking up a two-week engagement at the La Tropique nightclub in Durban. Unmoved by their cries of dismay, she summoned her mother Irene from Cape Town and put her in charge of the children, and Albert.

From the moment Josie boarded the train, Albert grew shifty. He spat out the pill Irene administered on her daughter's instruction, and by teatime was roaring drunk and waving a meat cleaver in the little yard between the kitchen and the annexe. Gerry sent the public barman out to deal with him. Oom Bubs was a burly Afrikaner with a gold tooth, skilled at handling drunks, and at least twice Albert's size. He hit the cook squarely on the jaw, snatched away the meat cleaver, and a jab to the stomach finished the job. Albert was carried to his room, and next day, hungover and sore, he packed his belongings and skulked off to the native settlement.

Gerry engaged a girl from the local cafe to help in the bar, and took over the cooking himself, but when the hotel's owners announced their annual inspection tour, his face turned grim, and Irene grew tearful.

Halfway through the second week, Josie materialised in a gust of steam and smoke as the train puffed away in the direction of Cape Town. She stalked into the hotel to find her husband perspiring over steaming kettles. Gerry's face softened as it always did whenever he caught sight of her, and he ran a palm over his balding head in a habitual gesture of emotion and uncertainty.

"The owners are coming," he said, rolling his eyes at the chaotic kitchen.

With her old sharp look back in place, Josie stowed her suitcase in the annexe and drove up the hill to the settlement. She found Albert squatting outside one of the huts smoking a roll-up, and wearing nothing but the filthy remnants of his checked chef's trousers.

Josie jerked a thumb towards the car's back seat, and Albert slunk over and climbed in.

"You'll take the pill?" she said.

Albert nodded. "Yeah Missus, I'll take the pill."

The owners arrived next day and Josie greeted them calmly, and with a perfect lunch. The hotel had never looked so good, and they offered Gerry a pay rise.

That night after dinner, the wife of one of the owners, a bird-like woman, leaned across and piped in Josie's ear.

"I remember how you sang for us when we came one year. I would love to hear you again." She clasped her hands, pleading for Josie to agree.

The flicker of bronze flashed once in Josie's eyes, and then vanished. She raised her plump shoulders, and let them fall.

"I've grown rusty," she said. "Let me order you a liqueur."

The Wasps' Nest

It had been years since Lily thought of Dorrie Brickle. When Lily heard her name again she was living in Broken Hill with her Brennan grandparents and their two unmarried daughters. She was there because her parents had wanted a better school for her – Lily hadn't minded the old one – but her father had insisted she was smart and the teaching was poor, and he had arranged for her to board with his family. Her sister joined her there after a year, but in her first winter Beth caught pneumonia and almost coughed herself to death. So their mother had come and taken her back to Wilcannia, and afterwards Beth's chest was deemed too delicate for her to live away from home.

With Beth gone, Lily had the long sleep-out to herself. The old people were kind, and her young and beautiful aunts, Sylvie and Grace, made sure Lily didn't get lonely. It was the youngest, Grace, who first took her to the store in the main street where *Brickle & Flacker: Quality Drapers, Haberdashers, Purveyors of Household Linens,* was inscribed in flowing script above the glass and polished-wood swing doors. Grace was running an errand for her mother, buying sewing threads for the greyhound rugs Grandma Brennan sewed in the afternoons when Sylvie and Grace were at work and Grandfather Brennan was stretched out on the lounge-room floor in front of the air cooler. In a town where almost everyone kept a racing dog, her rugs were in great demand. Lily would come in from school and find her grandmother hunched over the treadle sewing machine, and to spare her arthritic fingers Lily would sit on the kitchen step and pull through the pipings for her with a bobby pin.

Lily stood beside Aunt Grace at one of the long wooden counters while a shop assistant measured out yards of fabric for another customer. When the assistant took the money she fitted it into a wooden cylinder that flew across the store on an overhead wire. It went to the cashier's office high up on the rear wall, and soon came hurtling back with the customer's receipt and change. This was called a flying fox, Grace said.

"That's old Mrs Brickle up there behind the glass," she whispered. "Edna Brickle doesn't trust anyone else to handle the cash."

Lily stared hard at the cashier. Only the top half of Mrs Brickle was visible – she was a big broad woman with fat shoulders and permed, reddish hair. Even so, there was something queenly about her up there, sealed behind the glass, only connected to the hubbub on the shop floor by the web of wires and the little wooden cylinders.

Before they set out for home, Grace took Lily into the milk bar for a lime spider. Lily poked at a blob of ice cream with her straw and watched it froth to the top of the glass – she was still wondering about the woman in the cashier's box.

"Our next door neighbours at home were called Brickle," she said.

Grace nodded her small neat head – a few weeks earlier she had swapped her beautiful long dark pageboy for a pixie cut, and although it showed off her cheekbones Lily wished she had kept the old pageboy, like Aunt Sylvie.

"That man who lived next door to you in Wilcannia used to own half the B & F store," Grace said. "He was Edna Brickle's husband."

Lily stopped stirring the fizzing soda. "But the woman he lived with was nothing like the cashier." She thought for a moment, searching for the words to describe their neighbour, hearing in her head the voice at the fence and seeing Dorrie's pale sheep's eyes. "She was short and skinny," she said, "with black frizzy hair."

"So Ginny said." Grace began to gather up her shopping. "That was Dorrie Flacker. When she left school she had ideas of being an actress, and she bolted to Sydney without leaving so much as a note for her parents – they were lovely people, Bob and Iris Flacker."

Lily was trying to reconcile this information with her memory of their neighbour.

"So Mr Brickle left his wife and married Dorrie Flacker?"

Grace slid down from the stool and smoothed her skirt, a signal that she was ready for the long, hot walk home.

"Well, he and Dorrie left town together." A note of reserve had crept into Grace's voice. "I never heard of any wedding," she said. "It wasn't that kind of relationship."

The heat hit them as they stepped into the street, and sunlight flashed on the chrome bumpers and trim of parked cars. Grace put on her dark glasses. By the time they reached the traffic lights Lily's shift dress was stuck to her back with sweat. While they waited to cross, Grace pointed towards the green-tiled entrance of a hotel across the street.

"When Dorrie came back from Sydney she went to work there. It was a rough old place, back then, and after a week or two she went and asked Mr Brickle for a job at the store."

"Why didn't she ask her parents?" Lily said.

"They weren't on speaking terms," Grace said, "because of the way she'd left. And besides, her father had a bad heart and never went near the store. Anyway, Dorrie demanded a sit-down job, and of course there were none, except for the cashier's position, and that belonged to Edna Brickle."

Lily thought of the little cups of money, and the smooth wooden handles the assistants pulled to send them whizzing along the wires, and a little shiver of envy rippled through her. "Did Dorrie sit up in the glass box and count out the change?"

Grace shook her head. "Mr Brickle put her in charge of the fitting rooms and she sat on a chair at the entrance, checking what people took in."

When she started grade seven, Lily's parents moved from Wilcannia to Broken Hill. They rented a house not far from Grandma Brennan, and Lily went to live there with them, though she still spent much of her time at her grandmother's. Since Grace had got married and moved out, and Grandfather Brennan had died, the old lady seemed diminished and somehow defenceless. Her house – previously a place of comings and goings – now felt empty, and at a standstill. Sylvie encouraged Lily to walk over in the afternoons after school.

"Just until I get home from work," she said.

Lily would arrive to find her grandmother furiously pedal-ling the old treadle, and yards of piping waiting to be pulled through. One afternoon, Lily answered a knock at the door to a tall young man in a tan sports jacket and open-neck shirt. When Lily let him in he removed his hat to reveal a crop of curling golden-brown hair.

"I've come to pick up my dog rug," he said. "Desi Brickle."

Lily left him standing in the kitchen and went to find her grandmother. The rug was wrapped and waiting for him on the old chipped bookcase beside the sewing machine. Lily lingered in the doorway to watch him open it and run a thumb along a line of stitching.

"If Sylvie decides to sell that chestnut mare," Desi said, "I might be interested."

Grandma Brennan retied the parcel for him. "I'll tell her you asked," she said.

Desi paid for his rug, peeling crisp notes from a wad he produced from an inside pocket of his jacket. Then, as he turned to go, he looked back over his shoulder and winked at Lily. It was only a wink, one eyelid lazily closing to conceal the eyeball, but heat surged up from Lily's throat and flooded her cheeks. Around that time she would blush for the slightest reason. Grace had promised her that she would grow out of it, but Sylvie had shaken her head and laughed.

"You'll have to stop eating tomatoes," she'd said.

Her grandmother, who had intercepted the wink, ordered Lily to go inside and put the kettle on; she was anxious to get her away from Desi Brickle, Lily realised, and wondered what she thought could possibly happen.

When Sylvie came home from work Grandmother Brennan told her that Desi had his eye on her mare.

Sylvie was unimpressed. "As if I'm going to sell her now that she's just coming good," she said.

Grandmother Brennan picked up the poker and opened the front of the old wood stove on which she was cooking dinner.

"Desi Brickle is a chip off the old block if you ask me," she said, stabbing at the coals.

At school, Lily asked her friend Raelene whether she knew Desi.

Raelene rolled her eyes. "Of course!" She leaned close to Lily and whispered. "He asked my sister to the drive-in and had his hand inside her pants even before the cartoons were finished."

Raelene's older sister Margaret was now married with a baby boy. Raelene and Lily had begun to babysit. Lily absorbed this revelation in a silence that was charged with the memory of Desi's wink. She saw again the triangle of smooth, tanned skin at the neck of his shirt, and the tawny hair at the nape of his neck where it tapered to a single curl.

"Margie got out of the car and rang Mum from the kiosk to come and pick her up," Raelene said. "But a few weeks later a friend of hers went with him and stayed through two feature films."

"What happened?" gasped Lily.

Raelene's voice was casual, but a tell-tale colour had begun to stain her cheeks. "She went to Adelaide," she whispered. "You know, for an abortion."

Over time, Lily gathered more fragments of Dorrie's story. From Sylvie she heard how one Monday morning, instead of going to her chair outside the changing rooms, Dorrie Flacker had approached the floor manager and demanded an audience with Mrs Brickle. She was shown upstairs to the cashier's office, where she could be seen by staff and customers leaning over Mrs Brickle's desk, staring down at her with those pale, alien eyes. Since Mrs Brickle was too busy to deal with receipts and change, the shop assistants paused the flying fox and business halted. Sylvie had been buying stockings.

Dorrie had left the cashier's office with her cheeks flaming. She snatched up her handbag from her locker, and left the store. No one knew what had passed between the two women, but that evening, after Mr Brickle's usual detour to the pub, he arrived home to find that his wife had changed the locks on their house, front and back. He knocked and shouted to her to let him in, but Mrs Brickle had refused. Desi was a child at the time, and his anxious face was seen by a neighbour at one of the bedroom windows, before the curtain was whipped across. After walking all around the house, calling and knocking, Mr Brickle gave up and walked back to the store, but those locks, too, were different.

Dazed, and a little drunk, he took a room at the pub. His wife would see sense in the morning, he told the barman. But Edna Brickle remained steadfast, and a day or two later he was seen driving out of town with Dorrie Flacker in the passenger seat of his old silver Jaguar.

Wilcannia locals passed along the gossip. Mr Brickle had rented one of the rundown houses on Reid Street. It was quite a come-down for him, but there was worse: from being the proprietor of a prosperous business he had taken a job in the office of the stock and station agent. Dorrie kept house for him.

After they moved away from Broken Hill, Lily's family would make the long drive back to see Grandma Brennan and the aunts during the Christmas holidays. But by the time Lily had left school and started work, her visits had dwindled. As well as an office job, she had begun singing at night in a wine bar; there was barely time to eat, sleep, and shower, let alone make the long trip west. Besides, the desert town with its streets wide enough to turn a bullock dray, its tin houses and sparkling slag heaps, felt more like a dream than a memory. But there came a day when the bar job folded, and the bass player she'd been seeing ditched her for someone else. Furious, and desperate to get as far as possible from these disappointments, Lily quit her day job and bought a bus ticket.

The night before she left Sydney she rang Raelene, and her old friend's voice down the phone line, its flat country twang, jolted though her like an electric shock.

"You'll be here in time for the Paddy's Day races," Raelene squealed. "Let's get scrubbed up and go."

Sylvie met her off the bus, slender in her tailored skirt and heels, her immaculate pageboy streaked with silver.

The racecourse where Lily had spent so many afternoons trailing her aunts was populated by a new generation of race-goers. There were fewer old timers smoking roll-ups beside the horse floats, more young women teetering across the grass in platform shoes, though the heat and the dust were the same. From a seat in the grandstand, Lily spotted Desi Brickle. He was walking away from where the bookies traded, heading towards a marquee where an extra bar had been set up. As Lily followed the progress of his golden head through the crowd she felt the flutter of an old excitement.

That day he came to pick up the dog rug and winked at her in front of her grandmother, she had wanted to say something to him, though she had not known what. Later, she had been haunted by the image of his darkened car with an unwatched film unfolding in its windscreen. At night, alone in the sleep-out, she had imagined being in the front seat of that car with Desi.

Raelene had disappeared, and Lily scanned the crowd for her friend's hot-pink fascinator. She would take a peep inside that marquee, just a quick look, and then she would walk down to the rails and watch the next race. Away from the shelter of the old grandstand, the warm wind lifted the skirt of her white dress and flapped it about her knees. Even from a dozen yards away, the bar smelled of sweat and spilled beer and women's perfume, and Lily immediately felt conspicuous, the only woman on her own. She changed her mind, was turning to go, when a hand cupped her elbow.

"You look as if you've just lost a week's pay. Which horse was it?"

It was Desi, taller up close. His features were not as sharply defined as they had once been, but he was attractive still in the knockabout style of country towns.

"I don't gamble," she said.

Desi grinned down at her, and suddenly the dress Raelene had talked her into seemed both virginal and too low cut.

"Let me buy you a drink," he said.

"No, really, I have to get back to my friend."

"Raelene's a sport," he said. "She won't leave without you."

Desi steered her to where an older couple were rising from their chairs. "Hang on to these seats. I'll be back in a tick."

He headed for the bar, leaving her to guard the table. He hadn't even asked what she wanted to drink. She could push through the crowd to the exit without him seeing her, Lily thought. She could disappear before he came back.

He returned holding two plastic champagne flutes. In one of them a strawberry floated, a tiny pink parasol anchored in it with a toothpick.

"Last time I saw you, you wouldn't have been old enough to drink," he said.

As Lily took the glass from him she thought of that curl at the nape of his neck, how it might wind around a finger.

"Cheers," he touched his glass to hers. "Your auntie told me your family had gone to live in Sydney."

Lily wondered which of her aunts he had asked, and when.

Desi did most of the talking, and later she would remember little of what was said. She thought of the night when she and Beth had counted stars – how Mr Brickle had been driven off in the back of the police wagon while Dorrie's body must have still been in the house.

Desi was telling her about a horse he was training, a pacer. There had been a rhyme that went around town about Desi's father. Lily remembered Raelene chanting it and laughing.

Willie Brickle felt a prickle
Iris Flacker scratched it.
His wife found out and locked him out
And then went for the hatchet.

After Mr Flacker's death it had got around that Dorrie was Mr Brickle's illegitimate daughter. Perhaps a doctor's letter had come to light, Lily thought, or the results of some test confirming that Bob Flacker was unable to father children. The revelation had driven Dorrie Flacker mad. She had confronted her biological father, and later, when he refused to publicly acknowledge her as his child, she had blurted out the truth to his wife.

There was a second champagne cocktail in front of Lily. Beneath the table she could feel Desi's knees close to her own.

"I once lived next door to your dad," she said.

Desi nodded. "I've always wanted to ask you about him, but never got the chance." He added, "I barely saw my father after he left home."

"I was only a child," Lily said. "I didn't know much."

For the first time since they had sat down, Desi had nothing to say. Lily's skirt, under her buttocks, felt crumpled and soiled. She wished she had not remembered that awful rhyme about his father.

At last Desi broke the silence. "We should go for a drink one night in town, somewhere quiet."

Lily took the second pink umbrella from the rim of her glass and twirled it between her thumb and forefinger. It had come out at the inquest that Dorrie had never liked Bob Flacker. He was a mild and pleasant man, but she could not abide him. Then, after he died, Iris Flacker had told Dorrie about her affair with her husband's business partner. Once Dorrie knew the truth there was no stopping her. She even changed her surname to Brickle.

People had always known, Lily realised, that Dorrie was Brickle's daughter. The town must have been buzzing with it; it was too small for a secret like that to remain hidden. But she had wanted too much, poor Dorrie, and she had not cared who or what she destroyed.

"Pick you up around six on Friday?" Desi's fingers brushed the back of her hand. "Are you staying with Sylvie or Grace?"

They would not go to the old milk bar where she had sipped lime spiders. Desi waited, watching her as she twirled the little parasol. And Lily thought of their mother making them count stars, she thought of pink ice cream melting in a silver dish, those simple distractions that had once had the power to keep her safe.

TWO

Bearings

I return again and again to the image of a busy highway, with a car pulled over onto the hard shoulder. Half-a-dozen men lean in close with their bodies pressed against the paintwork, heads under the raised bonnet. The female driver stands mutely to one side, and though outwardly calm, body language betrays her wretchedness. From time to time one of the men asks the woman to get into the driver's seat, and to turn the key in the ignition when he gives her the nod. When she does this the stalled car momentarily stutters into life, although each time the engine sounds a little weaker. The men persist; they make further adjustments, all futile. The woman stares into the oncoming tide of cars, fortunate strangers getting on with their lives, until, with a final shake of the head, one of the men walks to his repair van and returns carrying a tow rope.

Now she sits behind the steering wheel with the car in neutral, while it is dragged towards a place where mechanics will use special equipment to discover what is broken. With no view of the road ahead, the speed of the vehicle she is tethered to alarms her; when it brakes she must brake too, or else smash into its bumper. This becomes her only task, a life and death wrestle: grip the steering wheel and brake, steer and brake. Trapped inside the useless, good-for-nothing car, her helplessness is demoralising.

This is as close as I have been able to come to writing about my infertility. While I was skidding along at the end of that rope I felt too raw to write, although I tried to keep a journal. Later, I thought that any account I gave might be marred by sentiment and self-pity; it would be too exposing and at the same time it would bore people. Even after thirty-odd years it still feels less risky to conjure up a broken-down car and a bunch of mechanics than to revisit the failure of my reproductive system, and the treatments administered by gynaecologists and IVF technicians. But what happened then with my body has become part of a longer personal narrative; it is also a small part of the narrative of women's reproductive medicine.

After six years of marriage, during most of which I was anxious to conceive, we started on the IVF program at Flinders Hospital in the winter of 1984; the date felt grimly apposite. In vitro fertilisation was a new and extreme form of treatment, the last chance saloon for couples who had tried everything else. I don't remember whether I knew then that the first recorded birth from an in vitro fertilisation had occurred only six years earlier. In England, Patrick Steptoe and Robert Edwards had pioneered the technique that led to the birth of Louise Joy Brown on 25 July 1978 at Oldham General Hospital, Greater Manchester. Australia's first 'test tube baby', Candice Reed, was born in Melbourne a little under two years later, on 23 June 1980.

Like all radical advances that eventually become common practice, IVF was controversial at first; it polarised public opinion so fiercely that after Louise Brown's birth her parents received hate mail. In the early days, Steptoe and Edwards worked without support from the Medical Research Council, which was concerned about ethics. It was said that 'The Establishment' wanted contraception rather than fertility treatment, a response to the widespread view that the world was becoming overcrowded. Hapless couples who could not conceive were to be the brakes on the population explosion.

People said cruel things to me about IVF, as they would later say cruel things about adoption. Unaware that we were on the program, a family friend, a woman of my mother's generation, said in response to a newspaper article about a live birth from a frozen embryo that the in vitro program was wasteful and should be stopped.

"Why would we want to reproduce these people we see being interviewed on television!"

I had to remind myself that she was also in favour of involuntary euthanasia.

"My husband would never have subjected me to that," she said, her face contorted with disgust.

She was widowed by then, but she and her husband had been childless, and I still wonder at the pain behind her condemnation.

It is my second morning of rising in the dark, this time to drink a litre of water before 7.30 a.m. The water is chilly and unappetising, but I manage it, and we drive to the hospital. My blood test causes trouble; the veins shrink from the needle, but in the end they relinquish a decent sample. The ultrasound scan locates two eggs, dark round shadows within my right ovary. It is miraculous to be able to see these raw materials of life, and their very presence makes me feel positive, and hopeful.

Day eleven: I am less buoyant. Hormone levels are not high enough, and an injection is needed to stimulate those tiny eggs. I have not yet started on the water treatment. They say they are holding off so as not to wear me out. In the early mornings, the same faces in the waiting room. By now we all have bruised arms from the blood tests. Tired from rising every three hours to pee, we clutch our boxes of urine samples, or sip water.

Day thirteen: the second day of liquid restriction. I am mad with thirst, and look forward to that litre of mineral water. In the waiting room, the woman who had three eggs collected has had three embryos returned and is now an outpatient, awaiting the result. Another woman had five eggs collected but only one returned. Yet another is pregnant. We are all stunned at the news, geared as we are towards failure.

Back at the beginning of my fertility investigation, which like a biblical plague would persist for seven years, a general practitioner in Hastings, East Sussex, referred me to a gynaecologist. In those days, in England, it was common for specialists to work from consulting rooms at home, and I arrived for my first appointment at a substantial Victorian house set in a rambling garden.

The doctor's wife answered the door, a pleasant-faced woman wearing a floral dress and a cardigan. As we stood together on the threshold, there were gunshots. I must have looked alarmed, because she hastened to reassure me that there was nothing to worry about.

"It's my husband," she said. "He's down the back shooting doves."

She led me inside then and up the stairs to her husband's office, where I would later undress and allow him to examine me. When he appeared he explained that they had just moved in and that the previous owners had left behind a dove-cote, and the doves refused to leave.

"Such a nuisance."

I have often wondered why I did not pull on my clothes and flee. Instead, at my next appointment, I would submit to the excruciating Sims-Huhner Test, the post-coital test for infertility.

The Sims-Huhner is used to assess the interaction between sperm and the cervical mucus. It is performed mid-cycle after a period of sexual abstinence. Then, after intercourse, and with no post-coital genital hygiene, the female presents at the doctor's surgery for sampling. The procedure is more or less identical to a Pap smear, with the sample being immediately transferred to a glass slide and viewed under a microscope.

Apparently the shortest recorded interval between inter-course and clinical testing has been ninety seconds, and the longest around seven to eight days. I was ordered to present myself to the killer of doves within two hours of having sex with my husband. The only upside to this bleak experience was that the doctor let me look through the microscope. The spectacle of sperm avidly hunting eggs made me smile – at least those little guys were wide awake.

One of the men this test was named after was J. Marion Sims (1813–1883), an American physician known as the 'father of modern gynaecology'. He developed a surgical technique to repair vesicovaginal fistula, a severe and deeply distressing complication of obstructed childbirth. He also invented the precursor to the modern speculum using a pewter spoon and strategically placed mirrors. To achieve his results Sims experimented on enslaved black women.

In Alabama, between 1845 and 1849, Sims performed surgery on twelve black women in his backyard hospital. Three of them – Anarcha, Betsy, and Lucy – underwent multiple surgeries, with Anarcha being operated on thirteen times before her fistula was successfully repaired.

Although ether was available as an anaesthetic from as early as 1842, Sims performed his procedures without pain relief. It was commonly believed at the time that black people did not feel pain as white people did, and thus did not require anaesthesia. When he operated on Lucy in the presence of twelve doctors, he experimented with the use of a sponge to wipe urine from the bladder. Sims left this sponge in Lucy's urethra, and afterwards she contracted septicaemia. Post-surgery, Sims administered opium to the women.

In the midst of the fertility investigations, a routine Pap smear returned a slightly irregular result. Alarmed that he would lose me to cervical cancer, my husband insisted I consult a Harley Street specialist. So I went up to London on the train, and reported to the great man's rooms. At this distance all I remember is the intimidating atmosphere, with him seated behind an enormous, bare and gleaming desk, and me in a small tub chair. When I asked him what the irregularity in my Pap smear meant his reply seemed to come from on high – perhaps even from beyond the clouded English sky. It was a 'pre-cancerous indicator', he said. Or something of that sort: I still didn't fully understand what it meant, or how it might have occurred.

He leaned forward. "Put it this way," he said slowly. "Nuns don't get irregular Pap smears."

Nuns? Did he mean real black-robed women belonging to a religious order, or did he mean 'nuns'?

Stung, I asked no more questions.

To my relief, we were on the verge of departing for Australia. Once there, I was admitted to hospital for laser surgery. In this treatment, a very strong, hot beam of light is directed at the cervix, and the abnormal cells are destroyed. Before they used the laser, and while I was under anaesthetic, the Pap smear was repeated and found to be normal. They lasered my cervix anyway, but I have often wondered whether there was ever anything wrong. Perhaps the pathology laboratory in Hastings had mixed up the results.

I have read that at the moment when a sperm penetrates an egg there is a tiny flash of light. In a natural conception this occurs within the private dark inside the woman's body. In a computer-generated film it appears both miraculous and utterly right. What else can this spark be but the beginning of consciousness, the light that persists until it is extinguished at death? Where it comes from, and where it goes, are the great mysteries.

In that winter of 1984, in a neighbour's garden in the Adelaide Hills, I was one of perhaps twenty adults watching a great many children as they ran and shrieked and danced around a bonfire. Sparks spiralled upwards through the frosty air towards the blinter of stars. Mulled wine warmed us, and eased the conversations between virtual strangers.

I had been chatting with a man who lived further up the hill from us. It's hard to imagine what we discussed, but we must have found something, as neighbours do. Finally, he gestured towards the children capering around the bonfire.

"Which ones are yours?" he said.

Soft hollow structures like the womb are difficult to X-ray. In hysterosalpingography a dye is pumped into the uterus and ovarian tubes; this dye, called a contrast agent, blocks X-rays so that the structures being examined show as white. A fluoroscope allows the radiologist to watch the contrast agent fill the uterus and fallopian tubes. In a normal hysterosalpingogram, the contrast fills the uterus, enters the uterine tubes, and spills out of the ends of these tubes into the body cavity.

In Adelaide I was sent for the test. A screen was tilted towards me as I lay on a trolley, and I watched the dye creep through my body until I began to feel uncomfortable. It was another of those moments when I should have pulled on my clothes and fled, but I was too invested in the result, too desperate to prove that my fallopian tubes were viable.

The dye was pushed at pressure against what must have been a blockage. It went on and on, until the pain became so intense that I almost lost consciousness. Weakly, I signalled that I might throw up, and an assistant handed me a kidney bowl. Still I did not protest, so badly did I want the result. When it was over, I could barely walk to the car. At home, I went straight to bed and did not get up for a week. When I did rise it was to go to the hospital, where I was put onto an antibiotic drip to treat a pelvic inflammatory infection that put an end to my slender hope of a normal pregnancy.

At 10.55 a.m. on 4 August 1984, at Flinders Hospital in South Australia, two tiny embryos are lifted from glass petri dishes where they have developed — one to the four-cell stage and one to the two-cell stage — and are transferred into my uterus via a long glass pipette. For the next three hours I lie on a hospital trolley, scarcely daring to breathe. I fear they may be expelled by even the slightest muscle movement — these precious embryos that are already our children. Can they sense, through the surrounding tissue, my tenderness towards them, my overwhelming desire for their survival? There is nothing I want more. Nothing. After three hours I am transferred to my bed on the ward where, even after I have been given permission to move, I remain on my back with a pillow under my knees. I must wait fourteen days to learn whether I am pregnant.

In *The Best Australian Essays 2016,* Tegan Bennett Daylight's essay 'Vagina' details her post-natal struggles after a birth in which her obstetrician resorted to using forceps and scissors. The epidural she had been given only dulled the contractions; it did not mask the sensation of instruments being manoeuvred into her vagina. Reading her essay, I thought of J. Marion Sims and the women who suffered in his backyard hospital without even an aspirin. Women's medicine has improved since 1849, although not as much we might have expected. Yet despite her suffering, Tegan Bennett Daylight gave birth to two healthy babies, and I knew that if it would have guaranteed the survival of our tiny sparks I would have taken scissors to my own vagina.

I was at school in Broken Hill when my brother was born in Wilcannia, so I only have vague memories of my mother when she was pregnant. But I do know that she often wore a straight skirt with a scoop cut out of the front to accommodate her stomach. There were no stretch fabrics then, so dressmakers had to be creative. Over the skirt she wore a loose, concealing smock.

Unlike today's proudly flaunted baby bellies, women in the 1950s masked their pregnant stomachs as if the sight of them would betray what they had been up to in the night. The language used to describe their condition revealed this latent shame. Women *fell* pregnant. They were, in a sense, fallen women. Needless to say, nuns do not fall.

In Broken Hill, my grandmother liked to knit in the evenings while she watched television. Her arthritic fingers, ever industrious, turned out exquisite little baby bootees. When they were finished she would stuff them with balls of cotton wool and store them in pairs in any small cardboard box that came her way. She stockpiled them to give as gifts to expectant mothers, and each time I visited she would tell me she was keeping some for me. Eventually, when the waiting had been long, she handed them over, 'just in case': a pair each of pink, blue, and white bootees, to cover all possibilities.

Having passed beyond the age of childbearing, my concern has shifted to wear and tear on hip joints and vertebrae. An MRI scan to inspect their condition detects something I have not asked them to search for. My doctor points to a shadowy area in the pelvis that I would, if I had a choice, avoid looking at.

"There is a large calcified fibroid in the uterus," he says.

"Oh!"

It is a benign, smooth, muscle tumour. He stresses 'benign' so as not to frighten me, but I am not so sure it is harmless. Later, when I summon the nerve to Google it, I will find that fibroids commonly appear in women during the mid to late childbearing years, that a fibroid can compromise an embryo's ability to implant. This is ancient water under an ancient bridge now, and I do not want to explain to this doctor how it saddens me, this useless growth. A year later, another scan shows that the fibroid has not changed, which I suppose is good.

"I don't want to hear about it," I tell him.

"Really! Why?"

"It makes me angry. I'd rather not know."

He is a kind man, and he persists. "Are you angry that it is there, or angry that you need to hear about it?"

"Both."

He gives me a look, and decides to let it go.

In the geography of grief, our deepest sorrows shudder through us like earthquakes. Pliny the Elder described earthquakes as 'underground thunderstorms', and in the language of grief these personal quakes cause seismic shifts and slides and thunderous collapses at the most profound level of being. Carrying grief is exhausting, too, and some days, by around three in the afternoon, I must lie down and close my eyes, or else implode. People joke about napping nannas, but it is the weight of the past rather than age that propels me towards the relief of sleep. All one can hope is that *gran temblors* don't occur too often in a life, or strike too close together.

I have experienced two actual earthquakes. The first was in Wellington; I was in bed at the top of the wooden house on Tinakori Road when I woke to find the furniture performing a strange slow dance. It took a moment to realise what was happening, as the little house shuddered at its roots, my bed rocked gently and the wardrobe door swung wide. The air felt volatile, and stretched, about to tear. I threw back the bedclothes, and everything fell silent. The room settled for a moment into that eerie silence, and then the second slow shake began. Should I run or stay? I clutched the wooden sides of the bed – perhaps the house would fold around me, and I would be buried alive on Tinakori Road.

The second time I was in bed in a *residencia* in Valparaiso, Chile, where the streets were already strewn with rubble from the last big quake.

Grief wakes up parts of us that we haven't known were asleep. Old griefs bed down beneath layers of scar tissue but can be laid open at the lightest touch. The chaos of grief caused by the loss of a child only ever lies dormant. As survivors of the female life we learn to bear up, for bearing up is the only option.

Time Passes

The two girls lay on their stomachs, absorbed in the colouring books Lily had found to keep them occupied while she dealt with lunch. They appeared quiet and companionable, but Lily knew trouble could flare at any moment – it was usually Belle who provoked her older sister, but Molly couldn't be trusted either. With their sharp little faces and reddish-blonde hair they reminded her of a pair of fox cubs. She couldn't risk leaving the baby with them. Rowan was almost fourteen months old, a placid, rosy little boy, who from the start had offered Lily his trust. Belle and Molly competed for her attention, but they remained guarded. There had been other nannies and from little things Belle had said Lily suspected that losing one or two of them had been painful.

With Rowan in her arms, Lily went upstairs into the public lounge, which was empty, and out through the main entrance of The Mariners Rest into Rye High Street. As always, she paused on the threshold, overawed by the age of everything in the old cinque port town, from the worn cobbles to the grey facades of the buildings. The George Hotel stood on the corner of Lion Street. Lily crossed to it and went up the steps and into the warm, beer-scented lounge where people had congregated around the open fire. The children's mother, Bet Levin, was not among them: Lily would have to look for her in the bar.

This ritual of drinks before Sunday lunch was a nuisance. It dragged Lily away from the kitchen just when the roast her employers required her to cook for them was at its trickiest. Once she found Bet she would go back and finish off the gravy; with luck, the vegetables would not be soggy. Bet's husband Gerald would drift in from somewhere just as she was carving the meat. It was a mystery how he knew when lunch was ready, but he always did. Once they had eaten, and the washing up was done, Lily would have the afternoon to herself, and she couldn't wait to take out her notebooks and finish the story she was writing.

In the entrance to the bar, two couples she had been introduced to by Bet called out a greeting. Lily waved but did not go over to them, worried that if they struck up a conversation she might muddle their names. The one with the moustache, who she thought might be Tony, saluted her with his pint of beer.

"Well, I must say, you look as if you were made to carry a baby on your hip."

Lily smiled, and her arms tightened around the child. Rowan must have felt this nervous squeeze, for he suddenly buried his face in her shoulder. His small warm body fitted perfectly into her curves, a barrier against this roomful of falsely jolly strangers.

"Bet's at the other end of the bar," Tony's wife shouted.

"Thanks!"

Lily moved further in until she could see Bet Levin perched on a bar stool. In her mid-thirties, slightly built but with a firm, boyish body, Bet was a strawberry blonde, like her daughters, and with the same sharp-chinned, predatory face.

She was laughing up at the man leaning over her, a fellow with a wine-coloured silk scarf knotted at his throat. His mouth looked a little loose. Lily thought she had seen him behind the counter at the gallery in Lion Street. Bet spotted her, and when Lily raised her hand to signal that lunch would be ready in ten minutes, she checked her watch and nodded.

A man sitting alone at one of the small tables at the back of the bar met Lily's gaze and held it for a moment: Thomas Raines. Amid the roar of conversation he seemed to occupy a quiet bubble that was all his own. Grey eyes, beautiful cheek-bones. She might put him into a story some time. Not like the story she had written about Desi Brickle, and really, she might scrap that one, even though it had taken her a long time. There was not enough in it that was true, and the one true thing – that Desi's father had died in gaol – wasn't there at all. The town was in it though, and her beautiful aunts, and the racecourse. How far from damp grey East Sussex it seemed, that dry-roasted mining town, and her grandmother's house where Desi had once come to collect one of her famous dog rugs.

Lily transferred the baby to her other hip, and Rowan gave her one of his brilliant smiles. When she had seen her own baby brother for the first time she had been so disappointed. Lily had pictured a playmate, someone nearer Beth's size, but Jam was a tiny blob, propped peacefully against their mother's shoulder.

"Is that him!" she had said in disgust.

Her mother had gone into fits of laughter then, letting Lily know that she was not going to take her disapproval to heart. It was not really his size, but the look on her mother's face as she held him that had cut through Lily. Ginny had never been able to disguise the helpless adoration she felt for her son. Beth, with her sensible, generous nature, had always been philosophical, but even now Lily was sometimes surprised to find herself resentful of their closeness.

When her mother returned to Wilcannia with the baby, she had sent Lily a red velvet dress with fake-fur trim. Ginny must have gone straight home and sorted through her boxes of dress materials, finally seizing on the red velvet as an offering worthy of her daughter's ordeal of jealousy and exile. And if anything could have eased it, the rich flurry of that red dress might have, especially the little fur muff that dangled on a velvet ribbon. It would have been perfect if the weather had been cool, but the town glittered with heat, from the dark slag heaps to the wide red strips that edged the melting bitumen of streets with strange mineral names – Cobalt, Chloride, Crystal, and the mysterious Brazil Street, which was always said with the emphasis on the first syllable – *Bra*-zil, which rubbed off the foreignness.

In those days everyone dressed for the races. Even Lily's grandmother plucked a pleated skirt from her wardrobe and eased her arthritic feet into good court shoes. When Lily appeared in the kitchen that Saturday morning wearing the red velvet dress, her grandmother had looked astonished.

"Now that's plain silly!" She had pointed at Lily's hands, hidden in the depths of the fake fur muff.

"Silly Lily!" Aunt Sylvie exclaimed. "You're going to roast."

"You'll get heat-sick." Her grandmother pressed her lips together, always a sign that there was more she could say but that she trusted common sense would prevail.

It did not. And by the time they left the house, though Lily kept a poker face, she was horribly close to fainting.

Her basement room at The Mariners Rest, with its single recessed window, was dark even in the middle of the day. Lily took out her fountain pens and notebooks – the room was like a cave, with small pools of light from the lamps; it was a good place to write. On the bed, propped up with pillows, she tried to think about the end of the story of Josie singing in the ladies' bar at the Santos Hotel, but all that came into her mind was the word 'Tinakori': *Tinakori Road.* She'd had so much time to write in that house, unlike now, when all she had were these precious Sunday afternoons. She could have written two novels there, at least, but instead she had sat in the kitchen, staring forlornly out of the window.

Tinakori was an anglicised blend of *tina*, which meant 'dinner', and *kahore*, which meant 'none', for the Maori labourers who had laid that road along the base of Tinakori Hill had been made to work without stopping to eat. Well, she had gone without dinner often enough when she lived there – that, and the exhausting grief after her father died, probably explained why she hadn't written more when she'd had the time.

In the week before Christmas there was a heavy snowfall. If Rye had been beautiful before, under snow it took Lily's breath; she kept going to the windows to stare out. Molly and Belle pulled on padded jackets and gum boots, and Lily helped them to build a fat snowman in the garden at the rear of The Mariners Rest. From their bedrooms they looked down upon his ghostly figure at dusk, and first thing in the mornings – carrot nose, potatoes for eyes, a straw broom under his arm, and one of their father's old scarves around his neck. The girls insisted on exploring the town, made unfamiliar by the snow. With the bundled-up baby on her hip, Lily slowly trailed them as far as the Gun Garden, where they could look out over the boats on the river, and beyond to the Marshes, and Rye Harbour: it was the snowy scene of countless cards that had adorned the sweltering Christmases of her childhood.

With The Mariners Rest closed to guests between Christmas and New Year, the girls played chase and hide-and-seek in its empty bedrooms. Whether it was the sheer number of hours they had spent with Lily, or having shared with her the potent magic of the snow, Molly and Belle had lost their reserve and accepted her wholeheartedly as their private property.

On Lily's birthday, Rowan took his first shaky steps towards her outstretched hands.

"Clever boy!" She swung him up into her arms, and went to find his mother.

Bet made a fuss of her son, but Lily could see that her heart wasn't in it. Ever since Christmas she had been distracted and jumpy, her face more secretive than ever. There was something bothering Bet, Lily thought, but perhaps she wouldn't ever know what it was.

In the Martello Bookshop, Lily bought *To The Lighthouse* and read it for the first time. Dear Lily Briscoe was her soul mate, and oh, how odious she thought Charles Tansley! But it was the middle section, 'Time Passes', that she read over and over. Every word of it was unbearable, yet Lily was mesmerised by its imagery of darkness and dust, stillness and light, the slow perishing of all that had once been so fully inhabited and alive. She felt it was the old house in Broken Hill that Virginia Woolf was describing for her, with her grandmother suddenly gone from it, like Mrs Ramsay. Or else it was the house by the sea where her mother had lived alone these last years; it was the house on Tinakori Road, and all the other houses that had ever meant something to her. And her personal time was passing too, dust accumulating as she cooked, and cleaned, and delivered Molly and Belle to school, and brought them home again. Dust gathering on her fountain pens, and between the pages of her notebooks, while she, like Lily Briscoe sitting alone among the clean cups at the breakfast table, could only go on watching and wondering.

Bet Levin was having an affair. At the tea shop in Lion Street she whispered this to Lily while Rowan dozed beside them in his push chair.

"The thing is, I'm going away with him for a few days, and I'll need your help."

Lily squeezed hot hands together in her lap and waited.

"I've told Gerald I'm going to London to stay with an old friend," Bet said, "but actually we're going further north. A lot further. Gerald won't ring the London number because he doesn't like the friend, and, well, that's what he's like when he gets on the wrong side of someone." Bet poured milk into her tea and stirred in sugar. "He'll expect me to call every evening to speak to the girls, but if he answers the phone he'll hear the pips and know it's a trunk call."

Bet was watching her closely, and Lily masked her nervousness by picking up her cup of steaming black tea.

"What do you want me to do?" she said.

Bet's sharp little face relaxed slightly. "I'll tell you what time I'm going to ring, and you make certain you answer the phone. I'll let you have a number where you can reach me, in case there's an emergency. Once you've picked up, you can pass me over to Gerald."

It was only the phone calls, nothing too terrible. Lily said she would stay near the phone at the specified times and pick up at the first ring. She imagined her grandmother's lips pressed tight, but common sense was pitted against the need to keep her job.

Afterwards, she pushed Rowan around Church Square and along West Street to Lamb House. Bet had told her that the writer Rumer Godden currently lived there, though it had once been the home of Henry James. Lily stared at the upper windows, imagining James's portly figure behind the glass. If she knocked on the door would Rumer Godden answer? And if she did, what could Lily say to her? That she longed to write a novel, if she ever got the time? Reluctantly, she turned her back on Lamb House, and as Rowan was still asleep she took the longer route back along Mermaid Street and up through The Mint.

On the evening of the day Bet left for London, Rowan focused his blue eyes on Lily and said, "Li! Li!"

"He's saying your name," Molly squealed.

The two girls gathered round, and Lily held the boy's chubby hands and smiled her encouragement.

"Say it again!" Belle ordered, and he did.

"Li! Li!"

The phone rang then, and Lily snatched it up. "Hello?"

She heard the beeps, and then Bet's voice, which even with the crackling line was tight with relief. "Lily! How is everything? How are the girls?"

"Everything's fine." Lily passed the phone to Molly and went in search of Gerald Levin.

Bet was gone four days, and on the last day Gerald stared coldly at Lily as she served his lunch. When his wife returned there were raised voices behind the closed door of their bedroom. Bet had been crying when she came to find Lily.

"Gerald tried to ring me in London," she said. "I really didn't think he would."

Lily sat Rowan down in front of his box of cars, and she and Bet moved into the kitchen.

"He knows that you knew where I was," Bet whispered. "Gerald and I, we're going to be all right, I think, but he won't put up with you being here. I'm sorry, Lily."

"But—"

"I know, it's completely my fault." Bet pushed her hands into the front pockets of her jeans. "I'll find a place for you to stay, and other work."

It had all happened so quickly, Lily's head was spinning.

She moved her few belongings into a room above the sweet shop next door to The Mariners Rest. Bet had got her a job at the gallery on Lion Street. After a month Lily moved to rooms in the High Street above Liptons. She was turning in there one afternoon when Bet and the children came towards her along the pavement — to Lily's dismay, Molly and Belle stared past her with closed white faces. Bet greeted her with an awkward smile, but it was clear she did not want to linger. Little Rowan leaned forward in his push chair, chubby arms reaching for her. "Li! Li!" he squealed, as Bet wheeled him away.

After Liptons, Lily moved to an attic room at Oak Corner. On the way to the gallery each morning she would pass Lamb house. She had more time to write now, but was still struggling with her stories.

One morning in late spring, when the wind off the marshes blew flurries of blossom over garden walls, Lily walked up Mermaid Street in a storm of pink petals and ran into Thomas Raines; he was standing in the middle of West Street, and at the sound of Lily's heels on the cobbles he turned and waved at her with the sheet of paper he was holding.

Lily saw that it was from a local real estate agent.

"I'm going to view a cottage," he said. "Its upper windows overlook Henry James's garden." He handed the paper to Lily. "Have you got time? Would you like to look?"

Before she knew quite how it had happened they were standing together inside a small but charming parlour. The agent came through from the back, and after a quick look at the tiny kitchen he led them upstairs, where they gazed down upon the famous garden. In the main bedroom, a blue Chinese bowl set in the window had been planted with white hyacinths. Lily closed her eyes and inhaled the scent. When she opened them she found Thomas watching her. She felt that he wanted to take her hand, but he touched her hair instead, which the wind had made wild.

"You've got blossom in your hair."

"Have I?"

"Just a bit." His gaze swept the room, passing over the hyacinths, the fireplace with its silvery over-mantle mirror in which the two of them were reflected, before settling on Lily. "Well, what do you think?" he said.

An image flashed through her mind then of a house that must belong somewhere in her future, its darkened rooms sweetened with the soft breath of sleeping children. There was a ticking inside her, and for a moment she fancied it ticked in Thomas, too.

Lily met his eyes, and smiled. "It's perfect, isn't it?"

THREE

Palaces of Loss

This summer, only a few days into a family holiday that I had been looking forward to for months, I began to feel homesick. We were staying in a small coastal town less than a two-hour drive from where we live; the weather was perfect, and the house – which we had rented the previous summer – was familiar to me and comfortable. Yet we had barely unpacked before I started thinking about home; it was as if I had left a part of myself behind. As we settled in and began to explore the surrounding towns and beaches, the silent rooms of our house would drift unbidden into my thoughts. I imagined the garden, too, with plums dropping from the laden tree onto the lawn, and birds coming unobserved to drink and bathe in the fountain. It was too ridiculous, this almost teary longing, and yet when I returned home a day earlier than scheduled it was with the same rush of happiness and relief that I used to feel on touching down in Australia after an extended absence.

The first sign that homesickness could kick in so close to home had come the previous year during a four-day trip to Melbourne. In the hermetically sealed glass box of our hotel room, which at night was almost too quiet, yet never completely dark, my dreams of empty rooms were weirdly reminiscent of paintings by Edward Hopper. As a long-time fan of Hopper's work – a taste that may not be unconnected to a susceptibility to homesickness – these dreams should not have been so disturbing, yet they were. Because the dream rooms were our rooms at home, standing empty in our absence, with their furniture and other belongings either missing or rearranged by unknown hands.

If I am to be confronted by visions of our house without us, I would prefer it appeared as if by the Danish artist, Vilhelm Hammershøi. At Copenhagen's Strandgade 30, Hammershøi painted a closed and private world of beautiful greys balanced against a complex and even more beautiful black; his solitary figures are alone at home, whereas Hopper's are often alone in public places, or in rooms so impersonal, so stripped of belongings, that they condense all the loneliness of hotel rooms. Hopper painted America mostly in saturated colour; he painted the night, with figures pinned under shadowless artificial light until they seemed drained of life. Even when the sun does shine in a Hopper painting, it falls heavily, except in his coastal watercolours, where it glints as sharp and bright as knives.

Hammershøi painted light as a precious presence. In his quiet rooms a square of sunlight falls upon the floor, a stretch of wall, or a card table, in images of mesmerising stillness and calm. But in Melbourne it was the Hopperesque vision of home that invaded my dreams, and the loneliness lingered on waking. I imagined the mirror in my study reflecting only stray beams of sunlight, or the infinitesimal accumulation of dust, and the section in Virginia Woolf's *To The Lighthouse* called 'Time Passes' came to mind. Although this is one of my all-time favourite passages of prose, there was something so wrenching about it in the context of home that I could hardly wait to board our return flight.

Meanwhile, friends were filling social media with photographs of adventures in China, Spain, England, and other countries. They were delighted to be 'away'; you could see it in dozens of smiling selfies. On our holiday to the coast I posted a couple of pictures of the sun setting prettily over the sea, and spent much more time wistfully scrolling through garden pictures on my camera roll.

Homesickness arises when we are unable to inhabit the same space that our memories occupy. What arrives then, if we are susceptible, is a creeping grief, low-key but all pervasive, that can produce symptoms very like those of depression. Having moved out of home at seventeen without a backward glance, I never imagined this would happen to me, and for many years, under the enchantment of new places and new people, it didn't. There was, though, a Hopper-like sense of isolation during those footloose years; I even worked as an usherette for a stretch at the Metro Theatre in Kings Cross, and Hopper's painting *New York Movie* evokes that time vividly whenever I encounter it. I was lonely then, but I was not yet homesick, being still at the stage of romanticising my life, endowing the future with limitless possibilities. But now, having reached an age when the future's limits are all too clear – and they are more than a tad scary – it is the present I engage with and strive to imbue with meaning, and the present is bound up in my sense of place, in being at home.

Friends promote the desirability of 'getting away'; the aim is usually to write, but also to unwind.

"You need to get away, Carol," they insist.

But what, I always wonder, am I to get away *from*? When

everything I treasure is gathered here under one roof, it seems beyond reckless to lock the front door and go, leaving it unattended. But perhaps what I am describing is a form of agoraphobia, or anxiety, or some other mental health syndrome; perhaps, if they ever read this, I will hear from concerned psychiatrists. For homesickness was once considered a serious disorder, and in this era of unprecedented mobility when large numbers of people leave home voluntarily for work, or pleasure, and others leave because home has become untenable, it is still a daily struggle for many humans. We see it at its darkest in the suffering of refugees, people who through no fault of their own no longer have homes they can return to.

The phenomenon of homesickness was identified in 1688 by the Swiss medical student Johannes Hofer, who named it *nostalgia* from the Greek *nostos*, meaning homecoming, and *algos*, meaning pain, grief, distress. It was the disease of soldiers, sailors, convicts, and slaves, being particularly associated with soldiers of the Swiss army who served as mercenaries and among whom it was said that a well-known milking song could bring on a fatal longing, so that singing or playing that song was made punishable by death. Bagpipes could do the same to Scottish soldiers. Deaths from homesickness were recorded, but despite various treatments the only effective cure was to send the afflicted person back to where they belonged.

The meaning of nostalgia seems to have shifted over time, from a sickness brought on by a yearning for home, to a yearning for a place and time that has passed and can never be recovered. Childhood is one such place – childhood, with all its palaces of loss. I am fortunate to still have access to two of the houses that were important to me as a child. Though the kings and queens are almost all gone, I was, at times, a princess in those places, and they belong to me, and I to them, in ways that are complex and magical. It takes time to build history with a place, although after ten years our house and I are getting close. Unfortunately, bonding forges a sword for us to fall on, and the Buddhists are quite right in promoting the desirability of a state of non-attachment. For whatever answers our deepest yearning is precisely the thing, that, when lost, will bring the sharpest grief.

At ninety-two, my mother lives in a house she first arrived at as a seven-year-old. Having left it as a bride, and returned as a widow, her bedroom now is the same one she once shared with her sister. But various illnesses have forced her to leave home for periods of time, to recuperate in my care. And although we make her comfortable, I sense the chaffing of homesickness, more terrible, perhaps, for the fear that she may never recover sufficiently to return to full-time residence.

Every morning, I walk past an aged care home, where framed photographs crowd the windowsills of single, functional, uniformly cheerless rooms. Some residents have brought a special chair from home, but there is little space to accommodate their personal furniture. For all I know the elderly inhabitants regard this place as a palace of comfort when compared to the terrors of managing age-related infirmities at home. But if homesickness comes when we no longer inhabit the same spaces as our memories, then this sprawling building is a palace of loss on the grand scale, a veritable Taj Mahal. As I pass along its southern flank, where no sunlight touches the bedroom windows, and the iron railings, though not above head-height, have been climb-proofed with sheets of perspex, I am grateful to be able to walk freely towards a café, and my morning coffee. The nursing home is a place of safety, no doubt, but it is also a kind of prison, and it reeks not only of overcooked food but of nostalgia in the modern sense of longing for something lost that can never be recovered.

It was while pondering the meaning of nostalgia and home-sickness that I was, by chance, introduced to the work of the Indigenous musician Geoffrey Gurrumul Yunupingu. Born blind in Galiwin'ku, on Elcho Island, which lies off the coast of Arnhem Land, around five-hundred kilometres east of Darwin, the acutely shy Dr G. Yunupingu (as he has been referred to since his death, in deference to the Indigenous custom of not using the deceased person's given names) was self-taught on a number of instruments. These included the guitar, which as a left-hander he played upside down but conventionally strung, thus forcing him to invent new chord patterns. His true instrument, however, was his extraordinary voice.

His remote community had already produced the influential band Yothu Yindi. Dr G. Yunupingu was a member of Yothu Yindi for a time, touring with them across Australia as well as overseas. Then in 2008 his first solo album *Gurrumul* was released to wide acclaim; over time, it went double platinum. It shocks me that I had never heard him sing until six months after his death, but back in 2008 I was studying, and pretty much everything passed over my head that was not related to my thesis, including, to my regret, this man's unique voice.

With limited English, he sang mostly in his own Yolngu language. But the language is lyrical, and his deep love of it is evident, while the beauty of his voice transcends the need to understand the words: Dr Yunupingu had, as many before me have said, the other-worldly voice one expects to hear from an angel. Perhaps the most perceptive comment about his singing was made by American music critic, Jon Pareles, in a review in the *New York Times*; Pareles wrote that Dr Yunupingu's voice "seems to arrive from a distance", and this is precisely what it does sound like – it is a voice that reaches the listener's ear from far, far away, perhaps even from a longed-for but irrecoverable past, for the voice of Gurrumul is nostalgia condensed. It did not surprise me then, when I searched for an English translation of his lyrics, to find that they almost all express the singer's deep yearning for home, and for his family.

"Grief have taken hold of me for my father, when the sun sets" is the opening lyric of his haunting song 'Bapa', about the death of his father. He talks about how, when the sun goes down, his mind goes there, to the familiar place. The song 'Baywara' begins in English, "I heard my mother from the long distance, making me cry".

To listen to Yunupingu sing touches the same nerve in me that Edward Hopper presses in paintings like *Morning Sun* and *Automat*, although Yunupingu's touch is gentler, more innocent: it is the touch of a child reaching for its mother's hand rather than the touch of a lover. His sublime voice taps into the same aching melancholy that Hammershøi captured in his silent interiors. Perhaps it is this common longing that all artists, in all disciplines, strive to identify and to match, yet it is accomplished only by the truly gifted.

Dr G. Yunupingu was admired by music celebrities, from Elton John, to Sting, to Quincy Jones, but there was something disturbing in the sight of this quiet, dignified, blind man appearing on English breakfast television. Gurrumul seemed vulnerable on the brightly lit set, and a little like an exotic specimen that had been brought from a strange far land to entertain. It made me long to put an arm around him, and lead him home. More surprising than his acceptance by music royalty, perhaps, was the positive response of white

Australians in such numbers to songs sung in an Indigenous language. Perhaps longing is its own language. Or perhaps they recognised in Gurrumul's voice the sound of a traditional man whose ancestry reaches back further than that of the kings and queens of England, and whose life was synonymous with his place, with Elcho Island, in a perfect symbiosis of man and land that those of us who are not Indigenous to Australia can only observe with envy.

In a sad footnote, at the time of his death in July 2017 he was said to be 'long grassing', or living rough, outside Darwin.

After almost two decades of living away from Australia, there were times when I feared that my homesickness would manifest as some unspeakable disease. I would wait too long to leave and find myself marooned; I would die in the place that was not my home. It was the light I missed as much as anything. In a television interview, the artist, Sidney Nolan, who had long been living in England, spoke about the special qualities of the Australian light; he wanted to spend his last moments on earth there in that light, he said. I cried when I heard that he had died in England during one of the darkest Octobers I could ever remember.

This preference for home over away is not fashionable. In affluent First World countries we are expected to aspire to travel, especially to exotic destinations – indeed, the conversations I overhear at the hairdressers hardly touch on anything else. To be what was once called a 'homebody' smacks of timidity, a lack of boldness that does not do credit, while admitting to homesickness on a ten-day jaunt to the seaside is scarcely believable and, frankly, a bit bonkers, but I am unapologetic.

What keeps me from travel is not fear – the world has always been dangerous – but the deep comfort of the familiar.

There *are* a few places I would leave home for, though it would be to revisit somewhere already loved and known rather than an expedition into unchartered territory. The heightened desire for home has, I think, to do with time – the way it appeared to be limitless when I was young and severely limited now that I am older. With that realisation, everything has shifted. I keep no 'bucket list', indeed, I despise the very idea. But what I do keep is a determination to draw every last drop of pleasure from the people and places I hold dear.

Changes of Address

She began to miss Tom the instant she lost sight of him waving from the observation deck. From Heathrow to Hong Kong the image of his raised arm waving a folded newspaper replayed in her head as she listed the arguments that had propelled her onto the plane. After two decades of yearning, she had given in to the long weariness of homesickness. These were the sacred words: jacaranda, oleander, eucalyptus. Lily recited them miserably, but was not comforted.

Flying over Australia in the early hours of the morning, the beauty of the land was gradually revealed by the rising sun. Lily rested her eyes upon luminous ridges of red sand; shadows of trees stretched slender fingers, softening contours that would be harsh by midday. Home. She followed the swirling lines and loops of dried-up riverbeds, finding not a straight line anywhere until the man-made scratches of a road appeared. The dots of trees gave the flat surface, with its snaking lines, the look of an Aboriginal painting, as if they had always known this terrain from thirty-five thousand feet. To fly for hours over the solid emptiness of Australia, she thought, was a source of comfort that was probably inexplicable to Europeans.

Gina slept beside her, her dark head drooping. She had shredded the past, Lily thought, and shuddered at the pain of the final days, of Tom's face as she crumpled paper to pack china into crates. Shaking, leaking doubt from every pore, she had climbed onto the plane, only buoyed up by Gina's enthusiasm. Gina still had not grasped the full flavour of their going; at thirteen her thoughts were of surfing, and swimming, and sideways looks at boys.

In the thick-walled stone villa where they had often been visitors, the polished floors were cool underfoot. Aimless as a sleepwalker, Lily drifted through the dim familiar rooms; although she had longed to soak in strong light, they had arrived in the middle of a heatwave, and the windows were protected by heavy curtains. Each night the house creaked and groaned in sympathy as she lay in the stuffy darkness mourning Tom. Through a stretch of scorching days it shielded them like a living skin, until the cool change blew in from the sea with a swell of net at the open windows. Then rain sang on the tin roof, and the wind roared in the chimneys and rattled the ancient sash windows, breaking the silence in which she sat, stricken. She and Tom had been parted before, but there had always been a date for a reunion.

Yet there was solace in inhabiting a long familiar space and she felt suddenly as if in all her restless life she had failed to find a pattern that matched this one, for it was this stone house that had established her concepts of space and light. Her mother's touch was everywhere, and her grandmother lingered, too — in the corners of the wardrobe, in the empty dressing-table drawers. Lily pressed a fingertip and gathered ancient particles of loose face powder, fine dust from the lives of the women who had inhabited the house before her. She would have been glad of their company and advice, but in the brown speckled glass she met only her own troubled gaze.

Their two suitcases, spilling clutter, had burst upon the orderly rooms like a pair of masked intruders. For all its familiarity she was a stranger here, and Gina, too, once the first ecstasy of running from the house to the sea was over, had discovered that she was a camper. Lily registered the discontented thrust of her chin towards a childish alphabet that hung above her bed, and the wooden horse belonging to some grown up cousin, which straddled the empty fireplace in her bedroom.

She waited for Tom to ring.

"I want to swim." Gina was fretful, with a whine hatching at the back of her nose.

"Just wait for the phone, and then if it's not too dark we'll go together," Lily pleaded.

But Gina's eyes flashed, and suddenly she was beyond reach. Exhaustion and the kaleidoscope of recent changes had catapulted her into that no-mans-land where thirteen-year-old girls, all jutting chins, elbows, and irrational impulses, run the gauntlet of parental displeasure.

"But I want to go now!"

"You can't. Not right this minute."

"You can't stop me!" Gina slammed out of the front door, and ran into the street.

Rage propelled Lily after her. "Come back now! You hear me?"

Gina's bare feet slapped the pavement as she marched stiff-legged towards the ocean. She wore bathers, and the straps across her back had slipped, revealing two crescents of paler skin: in the twenty-four hours since their arrival, Gina's olive complexion had responded to the sun.

Lily lunged forward and caught her arm.

"Leave me alone!" Gina pulled back hard, and pushed her chin forward into the space between them.

Still Lily clung to her; she even managed to drag her a few inches in the direction of the house, before Gina's strength and defiance defeated her. Panic and shame rose like floodwaters, as Gina flicked her hair and stalked away towards the beach.

In the bedroom, licking tears from her lips, Lily dialled the series of numbers that would connect her with Tom. As she listened to his telephone ringing, the front door clicked softly: Gina had returned.

"Give it time Lily, you've only just arrived," Tom said.

Choking on tears, she thrust the telephone towards her daughter.

"Daddy, I want to come home," Gina cried, as Lily wandered out into the darkened garden.

Tom's voice had sounded as warm and steady as always. She lifted her face to the canopy of leaves rustling overhead – she had left her husband for a jacaranda tree in flower.

At Brighton station where, as a schoolgirl, she had waited sitting on a brown Globite school-case, she bought a ticket from the Italian in the kiosk.

Hairy forearms reached across the counter for the money. "'s a dollar sixty."

From the train she gazed with dismay upon rows of utilitarian houses, broad bands of traffic, bus shelters disfigured with graffiti. She remembered with a pang the narrow house on the quayside, so recently abandoned – its winding stair, cast iron fireplaces, and tall shuttered windows. She mustn't think of it.

But what would have happened if she and Tom had never met, had never gone to the Isle of Man? She would have come home years ago, but to what? Would she be poring over plans for one of these dull brick houses on some suburban block, plotting to cover the space between plants in the landscaped front yard with bark chips or designer pebbles? She used to dream of a garden with orange and lemon trees, peaches, apricots, old-fashioned roses, and topiary birds in faded terracotta pots.

In the side streets of the city, she searched out its espresso heart. At Caffè Buongiorno couples crowded the outside tables, smoking, sipping strong black coffee. Inside, with the hissing Gaggia, the tubs of gelati, and the roar of conversations held at full throttle, it could have been anywhere in Italy. In a sad trance, she listened to the rise and fall of her own language, words she had not heard in years leaping out at her, recovered in a split second with shades of meaning intact. It was a convivial atmosphere, and in the espresso desert of the north of England there was hardly one such place. Perhaps, she thought wistfully, she might live like a migratory bird, departing at the end of each cool northern summer to beat her way south.

In the mornings, while the pavements rested in the shade of the houses, she walked, casting greedy eyes over ranks of white standard roses and the deep verandahs of Federation villas. In back lanes she discovered the wild gardens where frilly hibiscus and vines lunged over ramshackle fences, where pomegranates dangled beside passionfruit and quinces. She paused to crush leaves and breathe the antiseptic scent of tea-tree, the pungent sap of the slender leaves of the pepper tree. Here were plants she had forgotten; lantana, plumbago, tacoma, the dazzling bird-like strelitzia, and dreamy blue heads of agapanthus, which conjured the image of her mother, Ginny, teacup in hand, on an early morning tour of the garden.

"Such agapanthus this year!"

For years she had imagined these plants belonged to the animal kingdom: hippopotamus; rhinoceros; agapanthus.

The hiss of sprinklers was the music of childhood, and she listened to it now with sad delight as she waited for a sign, something to tell her what to do about her grief.

In the late afternoon, she and Gina walked the length of the esplanade where new houses jostled for elbow room; it had been all sand hills when Lily was a child. She shaded her eyes and searched the cliff face at the end of the bay where her aunt's old house, embedded in vines and trees, perched above the dry gullies – the gullies were now crammed with gaunt structures of glass and steel. They passed a rare piece of vacant land covered with pig-face and clumps of bunny tails.

"It used to be like this all over," she said, but Gina had no interest in the past.

A tiny dog materialised at their feet, a poodle, wagging its stump of tail and panting in the heat.

"Where did you come from?" Lily bent to pat its curly head.

A girl jogged past on the other side of the road. "Not mine," she shouted, and kept on running.

Gina stooped to pick up the dog. "He isn't wearing a collar."

In the creature's soft bewildered eyes Lily met the trusting gaze of her own dog, Cosy. Cosy had been left on the island with Tom, and was no doubt probing the chilly air for clues to the vexing problem of their absence. Her little footpads were tough from running on the shingle beach in all weathers. For days now she would have run and run, chasing seabirds, breasting sudden swells of icy salt water, and looking back to find only the lone figure of Tom leaning into the wind on the few yards of frozen sand at the water's edge. In the solid heat of a summer afternoon Lily shivered at the image of those solitary shapes, man and dog pressed beneath the marble slab of a winter sky.

Gina cradled the stray dog with the same enslaved expression she had worn when she came home from the boating lake carrying a rescued duckling. Lily's response now was the same.

"Gina, we can't keep it."

"Well we can't just let him get run over!" Gina's voice was spangled with overtones; the everyday teenage irritation she felt towards Lily, and the polarised opinions she held about liking where she was and yet feeling uprooted.

Behind them, a woman in baseball cap and trainers ushered a white standard poodle onto the pavement, then turned to them with a relieved smile.

"I've been terribly worried about this little fellow. I saw him from my window, darting amongst the traffic."

"He's not ours," Lily said, registering a creeping desperation in her voice.

"He hasn't got a collar." Gina still hugged the dog protectively.

"He looks very well cared for." The woman was a neat greying blonde who had powdered her nose with care before stepping out on her walk. "He must have escaped."

"We can't take it," Lily said, "we've only just arrived."

"Oh! Well, welcome to Adelaide!"

"He needs a drink," Gina said.

Lily closed her eyes against the enamelled glare of the day, and the sight of her daughter cradling the stray dog so tenderly.

"Keep an eye on Angeline and I'll find a lead and collar."

The woman pronounced her dog's name 'On-gel-een' and pressed the lead into Lily's hand.

Angeline swivelled plaintive eyes after her departing mistress, while on the other side of the road two women passed by, one of them with a miniature poodle on a lead.

Lily waved at them. "Do you know who owns this little one?" she cried, eager to divert Gina to the search for the dog's rightful owner.

The women crossed over, and Angeline lunged forward.

"BJ, behave!"

She and Gina were surrounded by white poodles of every size.

"There's a house further along where a little white dog sits in the window," said BJ's owner. "This looks like the dog."

"Someone will be heartbroken," said her companion.

Lily glanced at Gina's flushed face, and away.

Angeline's mistress returned. "I've found a lead but I had a little trouble with the collar."

Angeline swooned towards the woman, as she produced a piece of twine and tied it around the dog's neck. He licked her hand in gratitude as she clipped on a lead, the familiar snick of a clip giving him a moment of reassurance.

Gina set him down on the footpath, and BJ leaned forward to nuzzle.

"I'll take him along and see if anyone's in," said BJ's owner, and Lily sagged with relief as Gina relinquished the dog to the two women.

"Tom, I want to come back." There, she had said it.

"Are you sure?" Somehow her husband kept his grip on sanity, even in extreme circumstances.

"You sound as if you don't care."

"I miss you, but I don't want you to be miserable and–"

"I'm so lonely without you. It's taken all the pleasure out of being here."

"How's Gina?"

"Oh, having a great time."

"Well, maybe–"

"It's not enough. I know that now."

At the other end of the telephone, Tom sighed. Was it relief? Exasperation? Without seeing his face, she couldn't tell. In her mind he was far away, sealed behind glass, waving the folded newspaper from the observation lounge at the airport. Every time he raised his arm she wanted to scream.

"I won't go back! You can't make me," Gina was gearing up for a struggle.

"But I heard you tell Dad you wanted to go home–"

"I meant I wanted to see him, I didn't mean I wanted to go back! I'm happy here. I'm saving up for a really good body board from the surf shop." Gina shook her hair, as if that settled matters.

Lily stared helplessly at her daughter, this child to whom she had longed to hand over her own sun-soaked childhood. At what expense had she wrenched back the past, and now Gina, grasping it firmly, had made it her own.

In the hammock, swinging in dappled shade, she made a careful list. *Souvenir de la Malmaison* (named for the Empress Josephine, another exile). The incense rose and the beautiful damasks; Hebe's Lip (creamy white, tipped with red) and *Quatre Saisons* (oldest of the repeat flowerers). She sucked the pencil and closed her eyes. The ropes of the hammock creaked as she gazed up beyond the leaves and the greenish purple globes of the ripening figs, to the jigsaw of blue sky. This was a dream list of roses for a garden she could, if she returned to the Northern Hemisphere, nurture as carefully as she had nurtured the memory of childhood.

She took out the letter she had written to Tom. It was strange to think that in a week this same envelope would drop into a letterbox on the other side of the world, and that Tom would place his hand where hers was now and gaze at the rolling stems and loops of her handwriting. Lily folded the list, slid it in beside the letter and sealed the flap, held it for a moment against her dry lips.

Cradled by the hammock, suspended in warm air, her eyes closed as she made the gradual drift into that dreamy state which was neither sleeping nor waking but was more restful than either. In this drowsy stillness, if she was lucky, she would find the entrance to that long thin country on the edge of sleep which was the only neutral territory she could possess, her only true home ground.

She waited for Beth and Jam. It was a rare lunch date, perhaps the only time the three of them had ever met in a restaurant. A stranger, smiling broadly, cut a path towards her between the crowded tables, and for a moment Lily didn't recognise her brother. Jam dropped into a chair and turned towards her a face that was the mirror of her childhood, with everything that had happened since scribbled lightly on top.

Over chicken salad she said how much she envied people who resisted the bait of travel, who had the ability to stay put and be content.

"Those of us who stay away too long are cursed always to arrive like strangers."

"Is it really very different there?" Jam had always been curious about foreign parts, though not curious enough to leave Australia.

"As different as Mars."

"Any chance of a permanent return to earth?" Beth asked.

Lily looked away from Jam's patient gaze, which so resembled their mother's.

"I don't know."

"Is Tom really against it?"

"When he came here, he couldn't settle."

Jam didn't press for details.

"The trouble is," said Lily, "I can't leave, and I can't stay. I'm an exile in both places."

"Surely there's some way," Beth said.

"I wish!"

It was her sister who spotted the picture in the card rack at Dymocks. "Look, this is you, Lily," Beth said.

Lily leaned over her shoulder. It was a reproduction of *The Drover's Wife* by Drysdale. In the foreground stood a woman, monumental, solitary, with her back to the drought-stricken landscape in which, in the distance, a tiny covered wagon waited. In a peculiar way, it did resemble her. The woman gazed impassively at the viewer; in her left hand she held a bag – it was impossible to know whether she was leaving the wagon or returning to it.

Lily paid for the card. As ever, when preparing to leave, she snatched at things she could take with her, as if with planning and careful packing she could squeeze the whole of Australia into her suitcase.

After lunch she kissed Beth goodbye and stepped out into the honeyed afternoon. High up, the sky was an endless blue gauze freeway streaming away in all directions. Above her head birds fluttered, while in her grandmother's garden ripe figs fell soundlessly into the long grass.

FOUR

Kissing It Better

It was in the newspaper, a story about a South American city where the authorities tidied up ahead of an international summit by shooting numbers of street children. I am not even sure now where I read it, but I was just emerging from the tunnel of a gruelling and unsuccessful IVF treatment and decided on the spot to abandon the next round in favour of trying to save at least one child who was already in the world. It was one of those swerving moments in life when everything changes.

Between the decision and the deed lay daunting quantities of paperwork and permissions, intensive language classes, and visits from social workers. But so ferocious was my energy, that within a year I was on a plane to Chile. In my hand luggage I carried an enormous Spanish dictionary and, pressed between its pages, a list of orphanages.

There had been little time to consider the practicalities before departing, but flying in low over the snow-covered peaks of the Andes I had a dreamlike sense of being engaged in a bizarre and dangerous mission, like a spy, or an Interpol agent. The switch to Spanish added to the unreality, but the strangeness of being understood was an unexpected thrill that kept me afloat as I settled into a hotel and made the first calls.

Within days I had slipped into a parallel universe where small children free-floated without mothers, where they were not bonded to carers, where they sank from sight in institutions, or bobbed along on the surface, surviving as best they could.

It was September 1985, hot and sticky, and the city of Santiago wore a brooding and dishevelled air. Back in March an earthquake measuring 7.8 on the Richter scale had hit Central Chile, collapsing buildings and ripping up the pavements, but the greatest signs of upheaval were political. Twelve years of General Pinochet's dictatorship had forged a volatile society where running street battles erupted suddenly and were resolved by force, with water cannon, with teargas, and sometimes with bullets. Curfews and power cuts were common. Army jeeps rattled through the city's streets at all hours and on Sunday afternoons the mothers of The Disappeared protested with placards.

In the mornings I rose early, sipped cup after cup of weak tea and fiddled anxiously with my hair and clothing as I waited for a reasonable hour to telephone or to make the next visit. Pregnant women can dress as they please, but it was nerve-wracking to think I might be judged unfit to mother because of unruly hair or unpolished shoes. My days were spent knocking on doors. Some orphanages were staffed by stern-faced nuns. The others were state-run institutions in the charge of harassed social workers, desolate buildings that I fancied leaked sadness into the surrounding streets.

Everywhere I was met with the same answer: yes, there were children, but none could be adopted. In a population without access to contraception, abortion, or social security, one social worker estimated there might be as many as ninety thousand children stuck in orphanages.

"No more than one per cent will ever be adopted," she said. "Some parents keep children in care as insurance, so that when they grow up they can come out and support them in their old age."

Small faces clustered at windows to watch as I arrived and departed. Standing on the pavement with my list, listening to their voices echoing around the playgrounds hidden behind high stone walls, it was a struggle not to feel discouraged. I was running out of doors to knock on when a contact turned up news of a baby girl in a city a couple of hours away up the coast.

At first sight the port of Valparaiso was so beaten up by protest and broken by earthquakes that it was a test of courage just to step down from the bus. Stray dogs roamed the streets in great numbers, they slept anywhere, as if dead, and the speed and spin of the local Spanish made every conversation an ordeal. The faded splendour of Valparaiso grew on me over time, but back then my first thought was for the unknown child and my second was to leave as fast as possible.

She was already eleven months old. Malnourished and with a shaved head, she was in a children's hospital, a tiny ward filled with light, its windows facing out over steep hillsides where the earthquake had carved a trail of debris amongst ramshackle wooden houses. She had no visitors nor any belongings and had been in hospital about a week, sent there by the courts to be patched up before being moved on to an orphanage where she would pass her childhood. In the hope that she would make a favourable impression on me, the nurses had drenched her in baby cologne. Simond's Golden Lotion. The scent raises hairs on the back of my neck today. But she had no need of perfume. Weary and vulnerable, with bandaged feet sticking out beneath the hem of a much-washed pink cotton dress, it only took one look from her enormous eyes and I was smitten. And yet our first meeting – conducted on hard chairs in the social worker's office – was awkward. We were not alone and with curious eyes following every move, our first physical contact was restrained.

What she had been through in the eleven months before I found her was a mystery I gave little thought to as I struggled to steer her adoption through the Chilean courts. Of course I knew she had suffered, there was the malnutrition to prove it. Less obvious was the inner damage, the deprivation of affection endured in the tough back streets where she had been born. The real clues, if I had picked up on them, were her silence and the shocking intensity of her gaze, the way she rocked herself to sleep, or reached for a bottle of milk with her feet: these were signs of her loneliness and despair. I later learned that babies of her age sit up, but she would topple and her legs could not support her weight, which showed she had spent most of her time on her back in a cot. But I was an inexperienced mother and these developmental hitches did not strike me as crucial. In my exuberance I believed that loving parents and a comfortable home would rescue her from all that had gone before.

The weeks were filled with uncertainty and frustration. There was the infuriating incomprehension of other people and later, the terror that some slip of mine, of the law, or fate, would prevent me from rescuing a child with whom I was already bonding at a profound level. As the legal process ground forward there were moments of doubt during which

I entertained wild thoughts of staying in Chile, far from my home, just to be near her. And as the hours we spent together totted up, she seemed to know that I belonged to her, too, so that each time I had to leave her we were both upset.

I had bought her a teddy bear for company and she was clutching it on the morning I arrived bearing the court order that would release her from the children's home where she spent her final days in care. I was too impatient to wait while the matron called a taxi and insisted on leaving at once. There were padlocks and chains to be undone and then we were standing on the pavement in watery sunlight, just the two of us for the first time. I ran with her in my arms, ran as fast as I could over the uneven cobbles of the street. Her tiny arms were clamped around my neck and as I ran – hugging the breath out of her – I whispered that from that moment on she would have two parents and all the love that she deserved and more.

There followed a time of immense happiness as we watched her learn to smile and laugh, to gain the confidence to cry in the night because she knew someone would arrive with a cuddle. From not being able to sit up unaided she walked at fifteen months, tirelessly, up and down the hall in her new red shoes, her tiny hand tugging us along hour after hour. It was as though, having been captive for so long, she couldn't get enough of movement.

For a few years it was easy to believe that adoption made no difference, that if anything, it made our family special. Certainly we could not have loved her more if she had been our biological child, but gradually, as she moved out into the world, it became obvious that it did make a difference. It made *her* different, when what she wanted and needed was to be the same as other children. We tried to let her grow up knowing the truth so that it would never come as a shock. But it was when she came home from school in Year One and announced that she had argued with her teacher about coming from my tummy that I began to feel uneasy. Still tiny, she was already being forced to grapple with huge unwieldy facts of life that she could barely comprehend.

And so it went on through the years of biology lessons and times when children were asked to take along a birth photograph for some class project. Suddenly I realised how much we didn't know, simple truths that other parents and children took for granted, like her birth weight and the time of day she had been born. These details may seem unimportant against a background of deprivation, but they are the seeds of identity and every bit as vital as survival in their way.

Later there were episodes of bullying at school. Gradually it took a toll. We spoke about it less at home and it was around that time that I admitted to myself that if I could be granted a miracle it would be that somehow she would become my biological child. Not for my sake but for hers, for the security and comfort it would bring her.

Facts that children can absorb at seven or eight take on a different aspect at twelve and thirteen and when the first rejection came it was like an electric shock. We were shopping for shoes and there was a disagreement.

"You're not even my *real* mother!"

Once it was out I saw that it had been buried there for years, a landmine waiting for one of us to stumble. I was shaking as I unlocked the car and we sat for a while in silence. Finally I told her I had been dreading this moment, but here we were and somehow we had both survived.

We had kept in touch with other adoptive families and the news that filtered through of exaggerated teenage problems –

drug and alcohol abuse, eating disorders, underachievement at school and violent behaviour at home – might have warned us. But we had brought up our daughter with full knowledge of her adoption and believed that we were home free. Somehow we failed to realise that just at the moment when her origins had become distant and fuzzy to us, our bright child was struggling to assemble an identity. From her point of view, the raw material was missing and the clues she had to work with amounted to nothing more than scraps.

A month before her sixteenth birthday, our daughter stepped off the school bus one afternoon, walked into the house and took to her bed sobbing. At first we thought it was a temporary upset, but when it continued through the weekend and into the following school week with no sign of abating, it began to look more serious. Friends and family didn't understand what was happening; we barely understood it ourselves.

"Why don't you make her go to school?" they said. But her determination not to return was absolute and in any case, she was in no fit state. It was the beginning of a dark time for us.

The atmosphere in the house changed overnight: it felt unsafe, as if some invisible malevolent spirit had taken up residence. This sense of danger was so acute that I could only sleep when my husband was awake to watch over her. It was winter and the nights were endless. During my sleepless vigils I began to wonder about her birth mother. We knew her name but not her age, nor the colour of her eyes or hair. Soon this unknown woman haunted me as she was haunting my daughter. In the early years I had acknowledged her with gratitude, but during those solitary nights my gratitude was transformed into fury. I totted up the damage our daughter had suffered as an infant, the disastrous lack of love and affection in the early months. I wept for hours on those nights and sometimes during the days, certain that if I had been the biological mother I would never have relinquished her. But all the weeping in the world could not help and what mattered was finding a way to foster a sense of wholeness in this much-loved child.

Our GP referred us to a psychiatrist, who turned up at the house in drenching rain one Friday evening when our daughter was playing loud music and smashing things in her bedroom. She refused to talk to him. Instead, we did the talking, unravelling the weeks of anguish and despair while he sat nodding attentively on the sofa. As a last resort, we proposed to take her on a visit to Chile and the psychiatrist agreed it might help.

The return to Chile was extraordinarily painful for all of us on many levels. At times it felt to me like being flayed alive and I cannot really imagine how it was for her. In Santiago, we checked into a hotel opposite the terraced gardens of Santa Lucia hill, where fifteen years earlier I had filled a lonely Sunday afternoon dodging the courting couples and families eating ice cream to reach the summit. Then I had gazed out across the city and wondered if some nook or cranny held a child in need of the love I was bursting to offer. And here I was again, this time stricken by the possibility that all the years of care had been for nothing.

People in crisis look for omens everywhere. There was a lipstick kiss on the wall of our hotel room, the perfect imprint of a small mouth on the blue plaster. The height of it, and the size, suggested a child and it seemed to me symbolic, a reminder that our daughter wished to draw a line underneath her childhood and was determined to reject us. With my head on the pillow the kiss was level with my face and I woke each morning to its small, mute, yearning goodbye.

It was a journey on which she expected to leave us and although this was not a realistic option, it was impossible not to feel her struggling to detach herself from fifteen years of loving. Our relationship was tested constantly and at times the tests were scary, like the moment in Santiago when she walked away into the crowd on a busy street.

The only accounts that I had read of an adopted child's return to their country of origin described it as emotional but rewarding. Reunions took place in a haze of goodwill, with the subsequent return home a forgone conclusion, and almost painless. Our angst-filled hours in various hotel rooms could not have been more different, but perhaps we are the kind of people who take such things hard.

There were spears of gladioli standing in buckets outside the church on our last morning, brilliant green bayonets with blood red tips. I remember looking past the flowers to the worn face of a woman begging in the entrance, the rattling cup she held out and her cotton skirt hiding the stool she had brought to sit on: poor as she was she had come prepared while I had not and after three weeks in Chile it was impossible to tell what tests had been passed or failed, what peace of mind lost or won.

On my first visit I had met a woman who fostered needy children. At least two of the children I had met on my first visit were still living with her and she had news of others. It was at her house that a five-year-old girl climbed onto my lap and pointed to a picture in the guidebook I had opened on the table. The picture showed a man and woman walking with a child between them. She ran a stubby finger across the faces and her own face grew wistful.

"*Una familia completa*," she said.

We met kids with cigarette burns and other deliberate injuries, the damaged offspring of prostitutes and alcoholics, including a nineteen-year-old who, as a small boy, had been beaten so badly for crying that he still refused to speak.

These were children who would not easily be kissed and made better.

It is the random element of the attachment that adopted children find unbearable. And yet the profound and loving relationships that sustain and shape our lives most often spring from random collisions. In my own case I have always believed that synchronicity was at work when I found my daughter and that no other outcome was ever a possibility for either of us. Yet I can see what she has lost. In our affluent society there is a widespread view of children adopted from poorer countries as having hit the jackpot. But whenever I observe a mother bouncing a small baby on her knee and note their mutual absorption and delight, I am reminded that our child missed out on the one thing that most of us take for granted. Children like her need mothers, but in a sense they will always have one too many, for the biological mother is likely to become a ghost that haunts them.

Seventeen years on from that first fateful meeting, my daughter would insist that she and I were close, closer than many teenage daughters and their biological mothers. And it was true. With her wicked sense of humour she could make me laugh more often and harder than anyone I knew. And she could make me cry, too. But that eleven-month gap remained a black hole in her life and therefore in mine. It had etched distinctive patterns into her. For an eighteen-year-old of considerable beauty she could never allow herself to be frivolous, even for a moment, and what she hated most of all was surprises. Yet somehow we battled through, and after a gap year she returned to full time education, with creditable results.

Of the families whose adoptions I tracked through the teenage years, all experienced severe disruptions to family life. But was it any worse than might be expected with a biological child? Most think it was, because adoption magnifies the intense emotions of those years and offers an excuse for acting out. Of our six families, one appears to have broken down irretrievably while the rest have shown the same resilience and determination others muster for biological children in crisis, convinced that failure is unthinkable.

While I am the real mother in the sense that I have raised this child, my daughter's separation from her birth mother is a wrong that will never be put right. It saddens me, but I understand the sense she has that her life will never be complete. An ordinary birth is greeted with joy and once the baby is named, registered, and the birth certificate issued, there are no unknowns, no blind spots. Parent and child are certain of who they are. But adopted children have no clear linear narrative to support them and although adoptive families long to manufacture happy endings, the fact that we are doomed to fail is one of the unacknowledged tragedies of adoption. Curiously, my daughter has always said that she would like to adopt children.

I am not a huge fan of the poet Khalil Gibran, but these lines from *The Prophet* seem to carry a special warning for adoptive parents.

> *Your children are not your children*
> *They are the sons and daughters of Life's longing for itself.*

There is no question that I would do it all again, but another time I would ask more questions, demand the kind of details that later might go some way towards satisfying the natural curiosity of a child. I would arm myself too, for what might come once the soft and fuzzy toddler years were over. Now that I have had time to reflect, I believe, as I did not before, that adoption is a terrible thing. But the truth is that more often than not the alternative is more terrible.

For adoptive and biological families, good days arrive as well as bad and to the thousands of children and adoptive parents just starting their lives together, I wish only happiness. But I would urge them to bear in mind that the ride might grow rocky and that when it does the important thing is not to deny what the child has lost but acknowledge it. Above all, never underestimate the strength of the bond that has formed between parent and child in the growing years, because whatever the child may say or think when struggling with the question of identity, that bond is tough and it is a huge part of who they are.

Only love is truly thicker than blood.

A few months ago a friend gave me another of Gibran's quotes, a grain of wisdom and common sense that might help adopted children when it comes to weighing up relationships.

He who understands you is greater kin to you than your own brother. For even your own kindred may neither understand you nor know your true worth.

The Borrowed Days

There were spears of gladioli standing in buckets outside the church on that last morning, and a warm wash of traffic along the Alameda. I remember dragging in a deep breath, feeling an ache in my chest as I struggled to open the great wooden door of the church. It was the lost photographs that hurt at that moment, treasured images extracted from my wallet and torn into pieces. I had seen them as soon as I opened my eyes – mother and child in fragments on the bedside table. Gina had crept in and left them while we slept.

When Tom and I came down from breakfast she was folding her clothes, the same ones, over and over, with a face as blank and distant as the sky. At the sight of those slender hands folding and refolding, flicking at imaginary specks of dust, I felt Tom's exasperation, his longing to bundle us into a taxi and head for the airport. But there was still an hour-and-a-half to fill.

I told Gina I would return to the church. For a few minutes I would rest in that place where for centuries prayers have been said in her birth language, and where even my poor Spanish would be welcomed by the multitude of saints lining the walls. It was a pointless gesture, I supposed, but I would make it anyway. To my astonishment, she offered to go with me. I imagined she was feeling remorseful about the photographs, but now I wonder whether she planned to disappear in the crowds on the Alameda – perhaps she had forgotten it was a Sunday morning.

Santiago's streets were hot and empty as we walked along the edge of Santa Lucia hill. After ten minutes we arrived opposite the Iglesia de San Francisco, where the clock face on its tower had been stuck at ten-minutes-to-two since we arrived in Chile. Gina checked her watch as we waited for the lights to change. Avenida Libertador General Bernardo O'Higgins is so wide that we had to cross in two stages, and she slipped her hand into mine as we made the second crossing. The lower walls of Saint Francis's church are painted a dark and ancient red, the colour of dried blood, the colour of the secret, inner chambers of the heart, darker than the flower vendor's darkest gladioli. At the core of the church is a courtyard crammed with trees and birds, where the clamour of the city is all but inaudible. I saw it once, long ago, and so did Gina, but she was only a baby and cannot remember.

"The garden belongs to the Franciscan monks. You have to be lucky and find the gate unlocked," a woman at the church's small museum told us when we visited three weeks ago.

On this trip we had not been lucky.

In the dim, wax-scented interior of the church, an organ groaned a few low notes before launching into a hymn, a psalm; blood streamed from the plaster knees of Christ on his cross; the blue-robed Madonna's exquisite face looked frozen.

We emerged with ten minutes in hand to walk back to the hotel, but Gina was so pale that on impulse I hailed a cruising taxi. The driver set off in the wrong direction – we were within walking distance of our hotel, and he turned the wrong way. Gina glanced sideways at me to see if I had noticed. We were moving fast through the light Sunday traffic, flashing past deserted offices, and shops with their shutters down, racing along a street I had never seen before. I leaned towards the front seat and repeated the name: Hotel Foresta.

"I – 'ave – lived – in – Canada," the driver said, grinning at me in the rear view mirror.

Gina's lips curved. Perhaps she thought he would take us lurching up a side street and, in the kind of swashbuckling manoeuvre we had grown used to over these weeks, pull up with a flourish outside our hotel.

In five minutes we were due to leave it for the airport: Tom would be pacing in reception and checking his watch.

"Where are you going?" I asked him in Spanish.

"I – don't – charge – you – any – more," the driver said.

He accelerated, carrying us deeper into a strange part of the city, while the meter ticked and ticked and a framed picture of Saint Teresa swayed on the dashboard. Gina leaned back and closed her eyes; her mouth was pressed into the satisfied little bow it can make when anything falls apart and it is my doing.

"*Mira…*" I leaned close to the driver's ear. I spelled out the name of the hotel and said to make it snappy because we were due to catch a plane. With barely a shift in tempo the driver swerved across three lanes of oncoming traffic, triggering a symphony of car horns, as we slewed away in the opposite direction.

We were five minutes late, but Tom was so relieved to see us that he made no comment, just herded us from reception to the waiting car.

Once we reached the airport we imagined we were safe, Tom and I; we were light-headed with relief as we clambered from the taxi and piled the luggage onto a trolley. We turned our backs on the snow-covered Andes that for once were not veiled by smog; we were too anxious to be gone; we were speaking too fast as we fumbled with tickets, with passports, and the last of the pesos. Mentally, we were already halfway home, halfway to Madrid – change for Barcelona, change for Manchester, change –

For the first time in three weeks, we took our eyes off our daughter.

Inside, the terminal was a great open pale-grey space of hard and shiny surfaces. Check-in was upstairs behind a long glass wall. Beyond the glass, taxis dispensed more passengers and luggage against a background of dry, tan, scrub-dotted hills where the heated air wavered and trembled. We wheeled the trolley to the Iberia desk, and joined a short queue. When we were waved forward, Tom leaned down to lift the cases onto the weigh-in belt. We were so close. I offered the tickets and passports, and that is when Gina touched my arm.

"I'm going to cry," she said.

I turned from the woman holding our passports, and looked into her eyes. There were tears, and her mouth was crumpled, just as it had when she was a small child. I imagined she was crying because she was leaving Chile, but really she was crying because she was about to leave us.

"I'll go to the bathroom," she said.

I should have gone with her, but there was the hand-luggage, and the woman behind the Iberia desk was checking us against our passports. Gina had chosen the perfect moment.

"Don't be long, then," I said, smothering anxiety.

Within seconds she had melted into the crowd.

Waiting for her, my mind rattled through the days we had just traversed, with their bizarre and endless clutter: the salesmen on the buses selling ice creams, wire strippers, gift tags, and the way bus drivers stopped to let them board; Pablo Neruda's house in Valparaiso with its ships' figureheads, its plates decorated with hot air balloons and women emerging Venus-like from sea shells, its jacaranda flowers that brushed the first floor windows; and his Santiago house below the zoo in Bella Vista, where his and Matilde's initials were worked into the wrought iron window screens; it had a pewter bar, and a secret door that led up to the bedroom; there was a painting by Diego Riviera of Matilde, its two heads representing her public face and her clandestine life as Neruda's lover during his marriage.

A chunk of amethyst had been set into the wall of that house but it had failed to protect them; Neruda was brought there after his death for the final goodbyes, though by then the house had been vandalised by the military – in his study they broke the long case clock, and Matilde refused ever to have it repaired. And how those gypsy women in Valparaiso had frightened Gina by grabbing her in the street, wild-eyed creatures, with thin brown arms and long flowery dresses; schoolgirls with heavy eyeliner and black pencil around their lips; cold bottles of *Escudo*, and the dogs, and more dogs, and the fish vendors in the street bent over tables strewn with fish heads, fish blood, fish guts …

"Where's Gina?"

I hurried to the public toilets to look for her, but she wasn't there. She was nowhere. Gina had vanished. Panicked, I waited near the Iberia counter with our hand luggage while Tom went in search of her. Through the long glass window, I could see a line-up of buses for Santiago and Valparaiso: I tried to remember whether Gina had any money. Tom returned, shaking his head, and went away again to look downstairs.

These were the borrowed days, I thought, what the Irish call *Laethanta na riabhaí*, the 'days of the brindled cow'. Oh, I didn't think it then, as I peered into the crowds for a glimpse of Tom or Gina walking towards me, because for those minutes that stretched like hours my dumb mind was incapable of thought. But later, on the plane to Madrid, and again between Barcelona and Manchester, with Gina sleeping safely between us, I ransacked my memory.

It had been a school project on Celtic legends: it hinged on the month of March borrowing the first three days of April, with their fierce and spoiling weather. And these days in the Chilean spring, in which we had struggled to reconcile our daughter with her history, corresponded with those dangerous days in the north, that treacherous pocket of time between the first and second months of spring.

The legend went that the old brindled cow had boasted that March could not kill her, whereupon March borrowed three days from April – days of frost and snow, and a skinning wind – that had finished the poor old cow. In Northern Ireland the tale was more elaborate, with nine borrowed days – three days for fleecing the blackbird, three days of punishment for the stone-chatter, and three days to kill the poor grey cow. Hadn't the first King James died in the last days of March during a lashing storm, 'The Storm of the Borrowed Days'?

As I had hovered near the Iberia counter, stiff with fright, Gina suddenly appeared at my shoulder. Her hair, dark and glossy as the wing of a young blackbird, was drawn back into a knot. Her eyes were freshly lined with kohl, and for a moment they held a cruel gleam that made of her a stranger, too knowing for her years. It faded as she looked at me, for what she saw was the face of the old brindled cow that had once been brave but had now been skinned.

"You thought I had gone for ever," she said.

And it was true, although as soon as she had appeared I affected calmness.

Tom returned then, and we moved together towards Immigration. But the borrowed days would come again.

FIVE

The Happiness Glass

> Happiness is the lucky pane of glass you carry in
> your head. It takes all your cunning just to hang on
> to it, and once it's smashed you have to move into
> a different sort of life.
>
> *Unless,* Carol Shields

On a Friday morning in October, 2013, I was sitting in a café
with a woman I had been mentoring through the writing of
her novel. It was our final session, and towards the end of it
she began to tell me the story of her family's grief. At the heart
of it was a daughter who had chosen to cut all contact with
them, though she still lived in the same city. Distress flared in
this whip-thin woman's eyes and fluttered in her hands, as she
confided the awful details of what by then had been a two-year
separation. I can no longer recall what I said as I listened to
her; I must have expressed sympathy, then finished my coffee
and left. And then, that same afternoon, our own daughter
left home without a word and vanished. In fact, by the time I
returned from the café, the wardrobe and the chest of drawers
in her room were already empty and she was walking away

along some unknown street pulling a small pink wheel-along suitcase. You could not write this coincidence into a novel. As the Irish writer John McGahern has said of life: *much of what takes place is believable only because it happens.*

The next afternoon, while reporting her unexplained absence, I wept in a police station. In the years that followed I would grow accustomed to weeping in public places, and to sudden collapses, triggered by this or that unbearable memory.

It happens that I am going through a period of great unhappiness and loss just now.

It must be fifteen years since I first read that opening to Carol Shields's novel *Unless*, but at any moment during that time I could have quoted its first sentence. It lodged in my mind, yet I had no reason to believe it held personal meaning. I appreciated it, and the rest of the novel, for what it was, and remains – the accomplished, elegant, understated prose of a writer at the top of her form. Unfortunately, as it turned out, it was also speaking to me of a time in my own life that was yet to come.

In the novel, Shields's writer character Reta Winter is suddenly stricken when her eldest daughter abandons her university studies and the family home to sit mutely begging on a Toronto street corner with a sign around her neck that reads *Goodness*. On that October day four years ago, which in memory is bleak, though it was mild and sunny, I found myself plunged into a period of great unhappiness and loss that in some of its aspects was weirdly similar to poor Reta's. With this shattering of the lucky pane of glass and the move into a different sort of life, I began to wonder whether when we read something and are particularly struck by it, it is because of a subliminal awareness that we are reading forward into our own future. Can novels foreshadow human lives? Perhaps, if the signs are already in place, we will be drawn to literary expressions of the probable outcome.

All cultures idealise the family. Whatever its shape and size, the family we belong to is a huge part of our identity, sometimes the largest part, and for most of us it is a crucial navigational point on our personal compass. Even families like ours that did not start out bound by blood but were formed by adoption mostly manage to hold together through rough weather and family crises. To have failed brings a special kind of shame. It is death by a thousand cuts without the pain relief of death, or death's finality. But like death, a family estrangement is hedged by silence.

Photographs that have stood for decades on a mantelpiece are quietly put away; people avoid the lost one's name as they shun the name of the deceased. But unlike the silence that settles after a funeral there is a beady-eyed quality to the silence around estrangement: within it there are murmurings about good parenting, and especially about good mothering, never mind the swarms of crueller judgements and darker suspicions. For losing a child in this ill-defined way can make other parents in the wider family feel uneasy. There is a sense of stigma, no less real because it is never articulated.

Yet figures suggest that family estrangements are more common than might be imagined. Research is scant, but in 2003 Relationships Australia surveyed 1,215 Australians and found that seventeen per cent of respondents were estranged from at least one member of their family. More recently, University of Newcastle academic, Dr Kylie Agllias, has claimed that around one in twenty-five Australian adults experience family estrangement at some time in their lives, and a 2014 study in the United Kingdom concluded that estrangement crosses all socio-economic boundaries.

The word 'estrange' has its roots in the Latin *extraneus,* meaning 'not belonging to the family', or *extraneare,* 'to treat as a stranger'. From Middle French comes *estrangier*, meaning 'to alienate', and this is the defining condition of estrangement, for one cannot be alienated unless one has first been held close, just as one cannot be estranged unless one has first been loved. Another necessary condition of estrangement is that the withdrawal of affection discomforts or grieves one of the parties. When the withdrawal is instigated by a parent, and 'to alienate' has the connotation of 'to drive off', they are often said to have 'disowned' their child, a word that vaunts a delusion of ownership.

I began this essay in that small wilderness of days between Christmas and New Year, a patch of time as removed from ordinary life as some semi-lawless outpost where almost anything may be said, or thought, or written. The last days of the year are also the run-up to my birthday on New Year's Day, which this year was remarkable for the appearance of a super moon. Having been alerted to this phenomenon via social media, I looked it up and found that not only is the first full moon of the year known as the 'wolf moon', but in 2018 it will be the first of two full moons to fall in January. The second will be the 'snow moon' or 'hunger moon' that would usually fall in February. However, every nineteen years the full moon skips February, thus the 2018 'snow moon' will become January's second full moon as well as a rare 'blue moon', which occurs every two-and-a-half years. A complete lunar eclipse will be thrown in for good measure.

The waxing and waning of the moon marks the passage of the seasons, and in the Northern Hemisphere full moons were named for the behaviour of plants and animals, or the weather. Medieval Europeans and Native Americans bestowed these names, of which I had only previously heard of 'harvest moon' and 'hunter's moon', which fall in September and October respectively. Now I learned that March, with its final full moon of the northern winter, brings the 'worm moon', for in that month the ground thaws and softens and earthworms rise, inviting the return of birds. Sometimes the March full moon was called the 'crow moon' because the sound of crows signals the end of winter.

The 'wolf moon' alludes to the hungry wolves that howled on the outskirts of small communities in the depths of winter. This image of wolves prowling the frozen perimeters of one's life feels like an apt metaphor for the encircling grief of family estrangement, and on diving deeper into moon-lore I turned up an astrological interpretation of the full moon on New Year's Day that stressed its opposition to the planet Venus. This aspect, it said, emphasised imbalances in feelings of love and affection, though the full moon was said to offer great potential for peace and forgiveness.

Learning these lovely old names for the full moon in the lead up to my birthday distracted me from the lack of a birthday message; the making and shaping of sentences then took over and, despite the difficult subject matter, I found a kind of peace in the cease-fire zone of creativity. Like many things refined by time and passed down to us, the meaning of the full moon's names has been compressed, but opens in the mind like a flower: the 'pink moon', 'flower moon', and 'strawberry moon' or 'rose moon' promise warmth and delight after the hardships of winter. Other common names anticipate thunder storms, fish, the trapping of beavers, and the withering of grasses, until the year closes with December's austerely beautiful 'cold moon', or the 'moon before yule', names that honour the conditions and rituals of the winter solstice.

Humans have always looked to the natural world for signs and omens, and the astrological interpretation set me wondering whether this super moon with its aspect to Venus had influenced my sudden compulsion to write about this painful subject. It was irresistible to wonder too, whether, if I could only muster the right words in the right order, I could – I don't know – change things, fix what had been broken, embrace forgiveness, or even effect reconciliation. One of the buzz words of the past twenty years has been 'closure', but closure in family estrangement is rarer than the elusive 'blue moon', and while most of us who are caught in its coils yearn to be reconciled, the chances of that happening are negligible.

In *Unless*, Reta goes into a cubicle in a women's washroom in a Toronto bar and writes on the back of the door: *my heart is broken*. It's an impulse she recognises as "dramatic, childish, indulgent, grandiose and powerful", but at once she feels a release of pressure, which she ascribes to having set down words of "revealing truth". I am guessing it is a similar impulse that lies behind the writing of this essay – in the absence of closure, it is an instinctive move to let some steam out of the boiler before it blows, and at the same time write something true, though not, I hope, self-indulgent.

Children find it difficult to believe in the lives of their parents before they were born. I find it hard myself now to recall the tenor of those days, but they were less structured than the parenting years, and more light-hearted than the present as it bumps along with its load of unresolvable grief. One difference between a birth and an adoption is, of course, that the child also has 'before' and 'after' lives. The 'before' period might be short, as in the adoption of a newborn, or long, as when older children are adopted from orphanages or foster care.

The period of our daughter's life without us was eleven months. I sometimes think that if I could have rewritten what happened in those months I could have altered her future, could almost have ensured her happiness, and perhaps our own. It is wishful thinking, and impossible, I know, but at least those first months of life would have been drained of the horrors that by her first birthday had made of her a silent and unsmiling child. 'If wishes were horses, beggars would ride', as my grandmother would have said, but I will never relinquish that particular wish.

For me, our 'before' life always anticipated her presence. There was a space waiting for her, and for a time she filled it. Now there is a space again. I try not to swim against the tide of memory. Returning to moments of lost happiness is debilitating, yet there are days when it is impossible to resist the backward glance.

There was a photograph; I think my husband took it one afternoon when he met our daughter from the school bus. It was late September or early October, autumn in the Northern Hemisphere; in a few weeks she would turn sixteen. In the photograph she walks towards the camera, and her long dark hair – casually twisted into a knot – is tawny with late afternoon sunlight; a school bag is slung over a shoulder, and she wears the dull green army cadet uniform that flatters her. She is smiling into warm light, relaxed and beautiful, held in a wash of gold like something precious sealed in amber.

We call it 'the last photograph', because it would come to feel like the final glimpse of a beloved face in the moments before embarkation for some perilous migration from which there would be no return. A day or two after it was taken she would step off the same school bus and fall into her bed, weeping. It was the first stage of a journey that more than a decade later would culminate in estrangement. Despite all our efforts, and the efforts of the people we called upon for help, something fundamental had shifted, though for a few years more there would be flashes of the child we believed we knew, the much-loved young woman who was to become a stranger.

The cultural assumption is that parent-child relationships will survive almost any conflict, that the parent-child bond, of all close ties, cannot be undone. The factors that secure its endurance are said by social work scholars to be biological connection, along with a familial web of obligations and inter-actions, and shared histories. The involuntary nature of family ties is often referenced in their research papers as the element that makes most of us feel that 'the family', even if severely dysfunctional, is a personal force of nature, and inescapable.

My heart takes a dive whenever I encounter this cold line-up, for as a family we have struggled to meet the criteria. Lacking a biological connection, we might have benefitted from a firmer network of family ties, but we were a small family whose adult members were from small families, far-flung in some cases, so that it was always difficult to define and maintain that web of familial connection. Then, our shared history had an eleven-month dent in it, and as parents we were volunteers – though this gave us a sense of being in it for the long haul; at no stage did our volunteer status suggest to us that we could resign our parental posts. But on examining the factors that forge endurance from the child's point of view, the first thing I see is that severance of the presumed-unbreakable parent-child bond: it occurred, as far as we know, when she was four days old.

In *The Primal Wound,* Nancy Newton Verrier asserts that children never really recover from the primary rejection. While adopted children everywhere will at some time in their lives hear the 'you are special because you were chosen' narrative, nearly all of them, even when quite young, will work out that relinquishment came first.

I am still haunted by the story of the 2014 death of a homeless man in Dublin. Jonathan Corrie died in a doorway on Molesworth Street, just yards from the buildings that house the Irish parliament. He was forty-three. A photograph of Corrie in the *Irish Times,* taken when he was interviewed some months earlier showed a fine-boned face honed to bleakness, its most arresting feature a pair of deadened and immensely sad grey eyes.

In the podcast of the interview, Corrie was well-spoken, polite, with patches of eloquence. But I could not get his eyes out of my mind – their frightening blankness, like a one-way mirror in which you would see nothing but your own reflection. I could only imagine that, while sleeping rough, with never a private moment, Corrie had turned his terrible sadness inwards for the sake of dignity.

It transpired that he had been adopted when he was around ten months old. He said in the interview that his relationship with his adoptive mother had been 'small', that they were never close. "Sad," he said. "Sad."

His adoptive father had been good to him, but he had died of Parkinson's disease.

Jonathan Corrie's family home was in Kilkenny, where he had been educated at a prestigious private school; he had been a choirboy in St Canice's Cathedral in Kilkenny. Yet from around the age of eighteen he had been troubled and homeless, only inhabiting a small flat once for a couple of days.

He spoke about the toughness of the streets, of never feeling safe. His most telling remark was that there was always a story behind an individual's homelessness, whether it was of a difficult upbringing, drink, drugs, or mental illness. Corrie himself had succumbed to a drug habit.

With the report of his death, the revelation of his adoptive background and family estrangement came as no surprise: the figures for estrangement are said to be even higher among the homeless than in the general population. I did not know these people, his family, yet I felt that I did understand something about how they must have been feeling, and if it had been possible to sit down with them we might have talked for hours of our common experience, crossing and criss-crossing the contested territory of parental love, and the delicate grafting process that adoption attempts, and often fails. I felt his adoptive mother's wretchedness, and the devastated landscape implied by that 'small relationship' Corrie described.

His story raises so many questions for which there are no answers. For example: can the family home have been so terrible that a slow death on the streets was preferable? Could death on a cold doorstep be less difficult than facing up to what went wrong in a childhood or within a family? If adoption fails to bind, how else should we raise abandoned children? Corrie's parents were described as good and decent people. They had bought two houses for him so that he might have somewhere safe to live with the young woman with whom he'd had two children, but Corrie sold both properties.

His girlfriend sometimes searched for him in the streets of Dublin; he was always in their minds, she said. Once, she and the children bumped into him by accident and gave him their phone number. They were there if he needed them, they told him. But Corrie never called.

Towards the end of *Unless,* Reta Winter solves the puzzle of her daughter's withdrawal and her bizarre behaviour; the moment of trauma is identified, there is a homecoming, and the daughter, Norah, is gathered back into the family. But in life, estrangement rarely hinges on a single event or turning point. Novels must work with structure, and reader expectations; novels end, while life goes on, untidy and shapeless, and indifferent to expectations.

In the long shadow cast by the walking-away of an adult child I had believed would be close to me forever, other relationships seem frail and tenuous. A few precious connections forged in childhood, my long marriage, are as deeply carved as a river flowing between high scarred banks, but the rest feel uncertain, contingent, best described by the sort of small connecting words Carol Shields used in *Unless* as chapter headings: nearly; once; despite; instead.

I began this essay under the full wolf moon's beam, perhaps even prompted by it. Have I written something of 'revealing truth'? Is truth even possible when memories are not fixed, and when even the happiest of them is not the solid slab of glass one imagines but is made molten and slightly altered with each recollection? Was the 'last photograph' really as I have described it – a moment captured on the cusp of change – or was change already in place behind the mirror-glass? Will the sight of schoolgirls with long, lovingly plaited hair always trigger regret, and longing, and tears? When will I cease to be haunted by Jonathan Corrie's eyes? And you have to ask, I do ask, what could we have done differently? Was I never, despite the fiercest love, equipped to be her mother? Did the woman who confided her family's grief recognise some subtle version of her life within the little she knew of mine? Will the rare 'blue moon' at the end of January, with its lunar eclipse, bring a noticeable shift, or the longed-for 'closure', to either of us, or must we await a 'pink moon', or a 'rose moon', in some distant year? Or perhaps never?

In this different sort of life there are no answers, only questions.

Because. Before. Until.

The Weight of Happiness

A nurse has arrived to change the dressing on Lily's shin. This one is Irish, with a face in which round eyes hold an expression of bright wonder, like the eyes of a baby, or a kitten. She moves without haste, checking the previous day's readings.

"Now, will you tell me your name?" she says.

Lily answers this trick question absentmindedly. "Lily Brennan," she says, although no one has called her by that name for years.

Some of the nurses frown when she gets it wrong, but not the Irish nurse.

"And my name is Frances," she says, and her voice doesn't change as she peels back the dressing and inspects the ulcer. "It's lovely and bright out today." Frances tears open a fresh dressing. "Cold though."

Lily's shin is mottled, purple and green, and still weeping. Yesterday she heard the dreadful Miss Fiddy stage-whisper to one of the cleaners that poor Mrs Raines's leg was not too good. The skin is as puckered and translucent as the onionskin paper on which she once wrote long letters home. Lily closes her eyes and pictures the wound flowering beneath the bandage: it has

131

a wicked sheen that reminds her of a set of Chinese rice bowls she once owned.

Lying back in her chair, time rushes over her like a river – it was in Wilcannia that her mother had cut and sewed a black circular skirt that was to have a deep band of embroidery around its hem. Through the silent stretch of desert nights Ginny had sat with her head bent over the fancywork, hanks of silk thread slipping from her lap like brightly coloured flowers. When Lily's father came home from a trip he would give a hand with the embroidery. They worked from opposite sides, heads close under the kerosene lamp, with the black skirt stretched across their knees. Textiles last, thinks Lily, and she wonders what became of that skirt – all their hours of effort.

The Irish nurse strokes her wrist as she searches for a pulse, and Lily surfaces out of the past with a smile.

"When this leg heals, I'm getting out of here," she says, surprised at her own certainty.

"Oh! And where will you be going?"

She looks into Frances's wide-awake eyes. "Why home, of course. Australia. Where else would a woman my age want to go!"

The nurse blinks twice and looks away. "That'll be nice for you," she says.

Lily closes her eyes again, while Frances wraps the blood pressure bandage and pumps in air. She sees the softly rounded hills at home, their summer grasses bleached against the flawless sky, and the pilot flame of her resolve burns brighter. As soon as the leg is better. She should have gone back years ago.

The blood pressure bandage wilts, sighing air, and Frances pats her arm.

"There, that's you done, Lily Brennan."

Lily is the woman whose daughter went away. Although she rarely speaks of Gina, everyone knows the story. Behind her back she is *poor Mrs Raines whose daughter went out one morning and never came home.* Many people, she is certain, believe in a monstrous secret that will one day come to light. For what else but some scalding private hurt could compel a daughter to leave without a word, without a note? What, after years of love and care, could make a daughter decide to disappear?

Her thoughts drift, as they often do, to birthday parties when Gina was small. October: the Northern Hemisphere autumn, with colours turning and the dark coming in early. What she remembers is the cheerful leap of flames in the fireplace, and plates of fairy bread, and star-shaped sandwiches. She always stayed up late to ice the birthday cake – once, a My Little Pony castle, with ice-cream-cone turrets. Her pleasure next day as Gina puffed her cheeks and blew out the candles more than balanced out her tiredness, for there had been happiness in the room at those times.

Even now, Lily struggles to believe that her relationship with Gina is over. She wonders what she and Tom could have done differently; most of all she wonders how a child so unstintingly adored was unable to absorb their affection, and she pictures their love in this failed transaction as something like the molecules in trans-fats, for which, she has read, the human body has no receptors.

Gina left without warning. Later they would learn of preparations made in secret – a small, roll-along suitcase hidden in a locker at the bus station, belongings sold or disposed of – but at the moment of her departure they were ignorant of their impeding loss. Once they realised, there had been the agony of waiting for news, she and Tom pacing the silent house, confused and disorientated. How many times had she opened the door of her daughter's bedroom and slipped inside to run her hands over the cold sheets, to stare into the empty wardrobe and inhale her perfume. In those first few days it had felt as if Gina had died. At around three each morning Lily would rise from bed, leaving Tom to sleep while she huddled in a chair in the study. Those nights had been bottomless, tormenting, waiting in the thudding silence until she lost all hope of light. Rescued by the birds, at their first stirrings she had tottered downstairs to make tea.

On the tenth day there had been a note.

Please, don't search for me. I want to be alone.

Lily has kept the single sheet of paper, although she has not looked at it for years.

She has lost the trick of sleep. It is a cruelty of growing old, and the one she most bitterly resents. Consciousness presses on her, so that the merest flicker of light or sound draws her to the surface, and she understands that she has been floating there all along, just below the threshold rather than coddled in the deep. Through nights as black as Newgate's knocker (as her mother would have said) she listens to the wind moan and whistle along the nursing home's grey-tiled corridors.

Avalon stands on Ramsey's windswept promenade. She and Tom would pass its gaunt façade when they walked the dog, and there had been no premonition then that one day she would gaze out from an upper window across the dull grey expanse of the Irish Sea. She was sent here from the Cottage Hospital to convalesce after a minor stroke. It was to be for a month or two, the doctor said. But recovery has not been as swift or as thorough as Lily would have wished, and there have been complications with mobility. The loss of her independence is a death of sorts, though she does not regret leaving the tall, narrow house on the quayside – the House of Lasts, as she thinks of it, being the last place she lived with Tom, the last place where they saw the old Gina.

That house had been Tom's model for the tall, narrow doll's house he had once built for Gina. Years later, some impulse had made Lily sink to her knees in the top-floor bedroom to peer in its windows – the little house had been left as if in the aftermath of a burglary, with its dining chairs flung down on their backs, the kitchen dresser upended and its collection of miniature groceries scattered. Lily had reached in to where the family of porcelain dolls, once kept busy by Gina, lay face down on the drawing-room carpet – the mother, the father, the girl-child. In the nursery, the porcelain baby was squashed under the cot mattress. Lily had set about straightening the dusty figures, positioned their cold white limbs so that they could balance on the righted chairs while she tidied the rooms. When she had finished she closed the door of the bedroom, and never went in there again.

She uses the hated walking frame to reach the dining-room. The tables are covered with cloths in faded pastels, and at one of them a pair of withered men stretch tortoise necks over plates of beef and mashed potato. They don't look up as she hovers in the doorway, but a woman with groomed, bouffant hair and a pearl-grey cardigan makes frantic gestures. Dining-room etiquette demands that Lily share the woman's table. It is impossible to avoid company.

"Sit here!" Miss Fiddy pats the empty chair seat nearest her own. "I've saved a place for you."

Lily smothers a sigh and hobbles forward.

Miss Fiddy's eyes are narrowly set and too small for her face.

"I'm glad your leg is on the mend," she says. "It's nice to have someone of one's own sort to dine with."

Lily considers her companion's tin-coloured hair; she eyes the wool cardigan and pleated grey flannel skirt, and wonders, not unkindly, what makes Miss Fiddy think they are alike. With her dampened, unruly curls, Lily feels dishevelled and almost dizzily unconventional. Even the string of amber beads she picked up at the last moment feels exotic and somehow risky in the presence of this pearl-grey woman – in all her life, Lily cannot remember wearing anything grey.

A girl with pudding-basin hair and podgy arms clears the men's plates and returns carrying bowls heaped with a chunky dessert. The men grasp clean spoons and set to work without a word. When the door swings shut behind the waitress, Djuna, the young, blue-haired nurse pushes through it; she has changed out of her uniform into a shocking-pink skirt over black trousers, and a top that exposes two inches of creamy midriff. Miss Fiddy's breath escapes in a hiss, accompanied by a warning nudge of her elbow.

Behind Djuna hovers a man in an open-neck shirt. His thinning hair has been slicked back with water, and the teeth marks of the comb are still visible. Dewy and exposed, his face has the appearance of a peeled fruit. Mr MacInerney, the retired mortician. Lily avoids looking at his hands.

"Ah, Vesta," he calls, "how's Mr Arkwright's Girl Friday today?"

He chuckles, and Miss Fiddy's manicured fingers contract into a fist. She lifts her chin and stares away out of the window.

"Uh oh," he says, "bad day at the office."

Mr MacInerney pulls out a chair at the next table. He wears leather slippers without socks, and Lily's eyes skitter over purple veins threading yellowish skin.

"Here's your dinners." The waitress, red-faced and sweating, bears a tray loaded with steaming plates.

"So coarse," breathes Miss Fiddy. "I don't know how Matron puts up with it."

Lily imagines she means the food, until she sees that the woman's baleful grey eyes are hooked on the man at the neighbouring table.

Djuna helps herself to a plate of corned beef from the waitress's tray.

"Oh, Milly," exclaims Miss Fiddy, "How many times do I have to say I want salad or vegetables."

The waitress rolls her eyes. "Your dinner's on the way," she says, "this is Mr MacInerney's."

"You won't put gravy on it," Miss Fiddy insists.

Milly's nose rises a fraction. "Of course not!"

Her face has a simple, naked look, and her button eyes wander, as if searching for something. Not for the first time, Lily wonders if Milly is quite right in the head. Her own plate is delivered, with two slices of purple beef in a pool of parsley sauce, surrounded by peas, carrots, and sprigs of cauliflower. Meanwhile, Djuna and Mr MacInerney embark on a conversation full of joking references to Djuna's hair and Miss Fiddy's vegetables.

Under cover of their laughter, Lily asks Miss Fiddy how she is getting on with transcribing her old employer's memoir. Last night she had heard through the wall the steady peck peck of her ancient typewriter, bequeathed to her, so Miss Fiddy has said, when Arkwright and Co. finally upgraded to computers. The sound had reminded Lily of typing at the kitchen table in the house on Tinakori Road, and fleetingly she had felt those spaces pressing around her, had sensed again that house's self-contained yet lonely echo.

"Oh, very well indeed," says Miss Fiddy. "Mr Arkwright led such an interesting life." Her grey eyes shine as she leans sideways and whispers, "George."

"Pardon?"

"George Arkwright. I was his personal assistant for thirty-seven years. We started out together."

Lily has heard this many times, but feigns polite interest.

"I found a file yesterday which contained the first letter Mr Arkwright ever dictated to me. It was the day I got the job. I remember he looked at it and said, 'No mistakes right from the off, Vesta. That's what lifts you above the common herd.'"

The old men push their empty plates into the centre of the table and unfold from the chairs, and as they shuffle out the door they nod a shy farewell. Miss Fiddy dabs at her eye with a handkerchief.

Djuna lifts her nose towards the kitchen. "I thought I smelled cabbage."

"Matron has a private menu, which includes cabbage soup." Mr MacInerney grins. "I gather it's the latest miracle diet."

Djuna nods in a resigned way. "We'll be smelling lots of it then."

"Oh, I don't know," says Mr MacInerney. "You know how fickle Beattie is. Her fads never last."

Miss Fiddy's head snaps sideways at his use of Matron's first name. "If you ask me, some fads seem to have lasted rather too long."

Mr MacInerney turns with a teasing smile, and the bristle of grey hairs in his sideburns shift as he leans towards her. "And which particular fad do you have in mind, Vesta?"

Miss Fiddy stares in resolute silence at a vase of silk flowers on the windowsill.

"I hope you're not rather indelicately referring to our Matron's insatiable sexual appetite," his voice is low and liquid, "which requires twice or sometimes thrice daily–"

Miss Fiddy leaps from her chair, scattering cutlery. At the door, she collides with Milly and a tray of dessert bowls.

"Hey!" cries the little waitress. "Watch out!" And staring after Miss Fiddy's retreating back she calls reproachfully, "You haven't had sweets yet."

Mr MacInerney's eyes glitter with perverse amusement.

"You shouldn't rattle her perch," says Djuna.

"Vesta tends Mr Arkwright's sacred fire so religiously."

"But you do go out of your way to bait her."

"I'm only trying to inject a little realism."

The nurse tucks a wisp of blue hair in place. "It's true her fella passed on a good while ago. I'd have thought she'd have accepted it by now."

"Ah, but there's the Widow Arkwright; Vesta has sworn to outlive her."

"Old Mrs A is over ninety. She might snuff it any time, from what I hear."

Mr MacInerney shakes his head. "Tough as old boot leather, my dear. A drop of arsenic in the tea is Vesta's only hope, I'm afraid."

Lily shivers. She has no appetite for the salty, bruised-looking meat with its viscous sauce. On the nights after Gina's departure she had often wished for death. In dreams, or more often in the depths of her shabby velveteen chair, she had explored the possibilities: something painless, swift, an efficient erasing.

"Why not put Mrs A's name up for your Snuff Club?" says Mr MacInerney.

Djuna shrugs. "She's not famous."

He leans towards Lily. "This child and her friends pay a dollar a week to a snuff fund," he says. "It's a list of people they expect to die, and when one of them does, whoever holds that name gets a little windfall of cash."

Djuna chews a thumbnail. "I've got the Queen."

To wish death on anyone is wicked and dangerous, thinks Lily. Wishing dreams don't count; dreams are beyond control. Her eyes come to rest on Mr MacInerney's long hairless wrists, and his nails, with their perfect white-moon cuticles. It is terrible to think of going on, day after day, among these strangers. Once, she would have written them into a story, but Lily has forgotten that she is a writer. No, not forgotten, but who can keep writing when life becomes weirder than fiction?

Lily's shin sets up a steady throb, a drumbeat of discomfort beneath the bandage that threatens to erode her resolve. Suddenly short on courage, she summons the memory of her Aunt Sylvie at a night trotting meeting, elegant in a tweed suit with a pencil skirt: Sylvie's horse has completed a couple of laps when it falls right in front of her. The horse coming behind falls too, and without a moment's hesitation, this aunt, who is then in her seventies, vaults a low fence onto the track and wades into the wreckage to sit on her horse's head and prevent further injury. When the crash squad arrives to relieve her, Sylvie stands up and strolls back to the stands. Lily reminds herself now, as she often has before, that she comes from a line of women who can wrestle down a horse and sit on its head, all without snagging a stocking. Ignoring the pain in her shin, she straightens her spine – if she can only concentrate, the leg will heal. She will ring her brother in Tasmania.

"Do youse want sweets?" says Milly.

Gina's twenty-first birthday passed, and still they heard nothing. Lily, hot-wired with grief, went with Tom to an office in Douglas near The Rover's Return, where a private investigator, Mr Naseby, wrote down all they could tell him about their daughter. Lily had not known what to expect of a private eye, but she supposed the bulky, ex-policeman, with his drinker's nose and dandruff, was better equipped than they were to discover Gina's whereabouts.

After three weeks Mr Naseby informed them that their daughter was in Manchester. She worked in a pet shop tending puppies and kittens, tanks of goldfish, and cages filled with small, brightly-coloured birds. There was an address, and Tom proposed a surprise visit.

"Let me go alone," Lily pleaded. "If it's just me, she might—"

There had been hours of queasiness on the Isle of Man Steam Packet to Liverpool, followed by a bus ride from the docks to Lime Street station. After an hour the train deposited Lily in an unfamiliar city. Its clamour and speed were overwhelming; its rain-lashed streets had a tough, industrial feel – after so many years on a salt-scoured island she was astonished at the sheer depth of grime.

Gina rented a single room in a student building. You had to ring a bell at the entrance and wait. It was late on a Monday afternoon when Lily rang, and Gina answered through the crackling intercom.

She opened the front door wearing tight black jeans and a batik print shirt Lily had never seen before; her face was moon-like in its paleness.

"I knew you'd come," she said.

Lily longed to gather her up and hold her close, but Gina stepped back into the gloom of the hall.

"There's no lift, I'm afraid," she said. "And quite a lot of stairs."

Her daughter's smile was tentative but not unfriendly, though her eyes held a new blankness. Lily saw that Gina did not care if they had suffered, and that there remained no vestige of the old mother-child body language.

Breathless from the climb, Lily waited while Gina unlocked the door of her room. Inside, feeble light fell from an uncurtained window onto the scarred surfaces of second-hand furniture and a narrow bed made up with plain dark linen. When Gina flicked the light switch, a single unshaded bulb illuminated an interior devoid of personal belongings. This was where Gina slept, Lily thought. This was where she now lived.

"I can make tea downstairs and bring it up," Gina said. "Or it might be best to go out."

She was thinner, and the shed kilos revealed her delicate bones. A short choppy fringe exposed the perfect arcs of her eyebrows. Catching Lily staring at the fringe Gina flicked at it with her fingertips, a nervous gesture, and her eyes, rimmed with kohl, grew watchful.

"The cut, it suits you," Lily murmured. She remembered the warm weight of Gina's hair in her hands as she divided and braided it for school. Not to weep required enormous concentration. "I would have rung first, but—"

Gina shrugged. "There isn't a phone." She went to the wardrobe and plucked out a black duffle coat. "We can find somewhere to eat along the Curry Mile."

Djuna slips into the dining-room towards the end of lunch and takes her usual seat opposite Mr MacInerney. When Milly delivers soup the young nurse hovers her spoon over the plate, a pucker gathering between her pierced eyebrows.

Miss Fiddy's hair gleams with lacquer in the ugly yellow light from the dining room's brass chandelier. To Lily's relief she excuses herself from the table after ten minutes, leaving her salad untouched.

"Mark my words," says Mr MacInerney as the door closes behind her. "Vesta Fiddy is up to something."

"She's not the only one." Djuna takes a paper from her pocket and steers it across the tablecloth with a fingertip.

Mr MacInerney unfolds the letter and holds it at a distance. "Oh, my dear!"

Despite Djuna's war paint – thick eyeliner and black strokes under the lower lashes that make her look as if she's cried wearing mascara – her face appears naked.

"When I first moved into my flat there were no curtains on one of my bedroom windows," she says. "The previous lodger had set fire to them. It was ages before the landlady bought replacements and in the meantime I was visible to all and sundry." She has a defiant look that says if people pry and see things, it is not her fault. "This creep's written to ask could I please leave the curtains open like they used to be when I'd get undressed. He says I'm spoiling his only pleasure."

Mr MacInerney hands back the letter. "Which he describes in graphic detail."

"Filthy brute!" Djuna screws the paper into a ball.

Yes, that's what was different about Miss Fiddy: there had been a look of veiled pleasure in her small grey eyes.

She will always loath the smell of curry. It returns her in a flash to that walk with Gina along Wilmslow Road, stopping to peer at menus in the restaurant windows and all the while thinking helplessly of the miles the two of them had travelled together without effort – the long haul flights to and from Australia –

and wondering how this single road lined with curry houses could feel so difficult to navigate.

Gina didn't seem interested in how they had found her. It was as if her life before the stark little room and the pet shop had faded, or been erased. Something was broken, Lily saw, something she had not known was fragile. How could she have been so blind to the brittle nature of their bond? Perhaps she had never been cut out to be a mother.

After the meal they walked back the way they had come. Lily waited outside a Pakistani grocery, among bins of fresh dates and pomegranates, while Gina went inside to pay for a bag of pistachio nuts. Before the return journey Lily would stay overnight at the Ibis Hotel in Portland Street. Gina walked there with her.

"Well, goodbye," she said. "I've got work in the morning, otherwise I would come to the train station."

"What about Christmas?"

When Gina did not respond, Lily began to cry. It was a mistake, but she couldn't help herself.

Gina put a hand on her arm, and her voice, though cool, was not unkind. "You shouldn't care so much about Christmas. It's only one day."

Lily fumbled for her handkerchief.

"I don't know why you came, just to be upset." Gina dropped her hand and stepped away from Lily. "Look, don't come again, all right?"

Nothing could have prepared Lily for the blow of those quiet words. She would rather Gina had shouted, shown some strong emotion, even if it was negative. Instead, she was cut through by this kindly admonishment.

In the bland hotel room, Lily muffled her grief in the pillows. Around two in the morning she pulled aside the curtain and looked down onto the empty street. She pictured her daughter asleep in the narrow bed, and remembered a night in the house on the quayside when she had gone up to Gina's room to say goodnight and found her weeping. Earlier that day Gina had returned from a school trip to Italy. At the airport, her friends had rushed through the arrivals hall and thrown their arms around their waiting families. They had been gone ten days. At thirteen, it had been Gina's first real separation from Lily, yet when she spotted her and Tom in the crowd she had not hurried towards them but looked as if she would bolt in the opposite direction. Lily had thought it was a desire to appear cool in front of her friends. But that night Gina had sobbed that she didn't have the same feelings as other people.

"You're just over-tired," Lily soothed. "It will seem different in the morning."

But now, staring into the empty street, she thought that Gina, in a rare moment of insight, had simply told the truth. It was not her fault that Lily had not believed her.

In the kitchenette where she grinds her coffee beans, Lily finds Djuna. The nurse stirs the dregs in a coffee pot and tips them into a cup; she looks young and vulnerable, yet she has an inner fierceness that Lily envies. Her own existence lacks reality and permanence. It's as if she is stuck in a routine she must continue with until she can return to her real life. But what is real life, and how will she get to it? She thinks of the Irish nurse, her astonishment that amounted to disbelief. Going back to Australia might be a foolish mission. But the leg is almost healed and she will have to make a decision. People will try to dissuade her; they will ask awkward questions.

Djuna has her own troubles; she will not question Lily.

"Have there been more letters?"

"No, but I feel as if I'm being followed. It's freaking me out, like there's eyes on the back of my neck all the time."

"That's natural, after such a letter. But it's probably imagination."

"Yeah, I know." Djuna's mouth curves in a sad smile. "I hear old Mrs Arkwright's on the way out. My friend nurses her." Her blue hair is hectic where a beam of sunlight strikes it, and her skin is as white and smooth as a new bar of soap. "It's weird to think of someone dying while you're going about your everyday business," Djuna says.

Gina, Lily thinks. *Darling Gina.*

Djuna drains her cup. "S'pose one day it'll happen like that for all of us."

"The Snuff Club's only amusing when it's strangers doing the dying." Lily instantly regrets how preachy and disapproving she sounds.

But Djuna shoots her a level look. "Yeah," she says, "I'm getting out before Queenie snuffs it and leaves me holding the blood money."

There had been a secret, though it was not the great family rift outsiders must have speculated about behind closed doors. She and Tom had adopted Gina when she was eleven months old, and they had never kept that hidden. What they had glossed over, for Gina's sake, was her early life, the deprivation. Their social worker had spoken of malnutrition and the absence of affection, but Lily suspected Gina's ordeal began much earlier, her veins flooded by the nicotine and alcohol coursing through her unknown mother. There could have been harder drugs, and the physical violence of the streets. Gina had entered the world a jittery baby.

Lily returned to Manchester, but by then Gina had left the pet shop. When she buzzed her room an Indian student spoke to her through the intercom. In the office near The Rover's Return another detective took Gina's details. This one was dark and weasel-like, and Lily dully wondered what had become of Mr Naseby. They were given another address, and then another, but the letters they wrote went unanswered. It reminded Lily of a failed heart transplant operation she had read about, except that in their case the transplanted heart had rejected the sheltering body.

A photograph her mother once posted to Lily inside a birthday card shows Lily as a child sitting on a picnic blanket in the shade of a fig tree. A doll's tea set is laid out before her, and the shadow of the photographer, the familiar shape of her mother, falls across a corner of the blanket. On the back Ginny has written a verse from the Christian Science Hymnal: *For all the good the past hath had / Remains to make our own time glad.*

It is true, Lily thinks, for how else has she survived other than by the joy already accumulated. In her love for Tom she has experienced the immense heft of happiness, but the sorrow of not being able to conceive a child, and later her widowhood, are an equal and opposite weight. On the day they brought Gina home Lily had felt as if she could fly, and now, all these years later, her loss is a corresponding heaviness. That's how life works. The weight of happiness decides the degree of misery you will suffer. Eventually, balance, of a sort, is found. Lily teeters, but most of the time she is level. And something quite small can tip the see-saw. She is considering this when Djuna arrives to take her blood pressure and check her leg.

"Frances is off with a cold," she says.

Under her makeup the nurse's face is weary.

"I'm wondering if it's one of my old boyfriends."

"Were any of them troublesome?"

"I was engaged once. His mother broke us up."

Lily says, "Didn't she like you?"

"I never wrote to thank her for some money she sent me on my birthday. You'd of thought she'd cut off her left tit and given it to me, to hear her." Djuna's mouth hardens. "He sided with her, even though she never sent a note for anything I gave her. When I brought that up she said she'd never been given anything she wanted." She lifts Lily's feet onto a footstool. "He should have stuck up for me." Her eyes shine with unshed tears.

Djuna's predicament reminds Lily of her own defenceless-ness, back in the time before she met Tom.

"Why not take those letters to the police?"

The nurse shakes her head. "Did you know Miss Fiddy's rival died yesterday?"

Lily remembers the pleasure in Vesta Fiddy's eyes, and wonders whether surviving her boss's wife will balance the misery of having only ever been his mistress. She watches Djuna's gentle movements as she removes the bandage. Lily has money, enough to fund the small measure of happiness that will tip the balance for herself, and perhaps even for this young woman.

"Djuna, would you ever consider going to Australia?"

The young nurse raises her face to stare at Lily.

From Tasmania, her brother's wife had not been encourag-ing. "Jam has his hands full," she said firmly. Their daughter was going through a messy divorce, and she and Jam had to be there for the grandchildren. Beth's husband was battling cancer: Lily couldn't ask her to help.

"I've been waiting for the leg to heal," she tells Djuna. "And now that it has, I'm going home."

"But—"

"I'll need a travelling companion," Lily says quickly. "If it appeals to you, once I'm settled, you could stay for as long as you liked."

She hears her mother's voice calmly reading the bible: *I will return into my house from whence I came out.* No, there would not be the comfort of those remembered rooms, but there would be no ghosts, either. Lily imagines a stone cottage with whitewashed walls in the leafy part of the city, a final spell of freedom before the need for another Avalon. She might buy a laptop and pick up her old pastime – that slow writing-breath that was once so soothing. Djuna will leave her, of course; it is to be expected.

The nurse's tears spill over. "What's it like, Australia?"

Lily's gaze settles on the sleek blue curve of Djuna's head. Home, in November, is a soft rain of petals; where jacarandas shed flowers on red brick paving the colours vibrate as in a Bonnard painting. She will speak persuasively of Adelaide's clear blue skies, the dry bright air she craves.

"There is no grey," Lily says, "and you would love the jacaranda flowers."

Acknowledgements

Some of these stories have previously been published, but I always knew that they were part of a longer, unwritten, autobiographical narrative. It wasn't until I had the idea of combining the short stories with memoir that the work finally came together. It was exciting to discover that combining genres allowed the fiction to deepen the sense of place, and further interpret the sometimes painful subject matter of the memoir. I realised I had found a way to manage some of the difficulties of life writing, and there was a playfulness, too, as the memoir pieces spoke to the stories, and the stories answered. As a writing process it has felt very close to the way that one's life and writing are always in conversation, the way they merge and diverge in a constant ravelling of lived experience and reworked story.

To be clear: each section begins with a memoir piece or personal essay followed by one or more short fictions. While the borders between the two are somewhat fluid, the life of Lily Brennan, told in fragments, must not be read as if it were my life. For while we have lived in the same houses, and shared some life experiences, there are significant differences, and Lily's stories are peopled with invented characters.

But what is fact and what is fiction? Where in a bookshop should *The Happiness Glass* be shelved? To pre-empt those questions let me say that the five memoir pieces, to the best of my knowledge, only contain what I believe to be true. However, any life, as soon as you begin to tell it, becomes a story; told from a single point of view, it can never be definitive. It is inevitable, too, that there will be gaps – of memory, of discretion – so readers who require certainty should treat the entire work as fiction.

Of the essays and stories, 'Kissing it Better' appeared in the anthology *Family Wanted: Adoption Stories,* edited by Sara Holloway, Granta (2005). An earlier version of 'The Stars of the Milky Way' was published in *Wet Ink* (2006) and an earlier version of 'Changes of Address' appeared as 'Homeground' in the anthology *On Edge* (Wakefield Press, 2005).

'Burning with Madame Bovary' was begun between drafts of a novel during a six-month writing residency at the J.M. Coetzee Centre for Creative Practice. I am grateful to the Centre, and to the Copyright Agency, for that generously funded fellowship, which gave me space and time to write. I am also grateful for the continuing support of The Department of English and Creative Writing at the University of Adelaide, where I am a Visiting Research Fellow.

Over time, friends have read and offered feedback on the stories, and in particular I am grateful to Gillian Britton, Gay Lynch, and Diane Schwerdt. Big thanks to my agent Fran Moore, and to Susan Hawthorne and Pauline Hopkins at Spinifex Press. Thanks to Dymphna Lonergan for her advice on the Irish language phrase in 'The Borrowed Days', and to Jason Hiscock for locating the photograph of Argent Street. Finally, endless gratitude is due to Christopher and Rafael Lefevre for their willingness to share my wyrd.

Other books available from Spinifex Press

Locust Girl, a Lovesong
Merlinda Bobis

Winner, Christina Stead Award, NSW Premier's Literary Awards

Most everything has dried up: water, the womb, even the love among lovers. Hunger is rife, except across the border. Nine-year-old Amadea survives the bombing of her village to wake ten years later with a locust embedded in her brow. She journeys to the border, which has cut the human heart. Can she repair it with the story of a small life? This is the Locust Girl's dream, her lovesong.

ISBN 9781742199627

The Floating Garden
Emma Ashmere

Sydney, 1926, and the residents of the tight-knit Milsons Point community face imminent homelessness: the construction of the harbour bridge spells the demolition of their homes. Ellis Gilbey, landlady by day, gardening writer by night, is set to lose everything. Only her belief in the book she is writing, and the hopes of a garden of her own, allow her to fend off despair. This beautiful debut novel evokes the hardships and the glories of the 1920s and tells the little-known story of those who faced upheaval because of the famous bridge.

ISBN 9781742199368

Ann Hannah, My (Un)Remarkable Grandmother
Betty McLellan

Ann Hannah, the author's grandmother, was an ordinary, no-nonsense, working-class woman, who was forced to migrate to Australia from England in the 1920s. What was the truth about her life, and the how did she manage to overcome her many struggles and disappointments? Written with a sharp feminist consciousness that displays both compassion and intellect, this is an astute psychological biography of a resilient woman. It provides valuable insight into the lives of many (un) remarkable women whose lives may have gone unnoticed but whose experiences shed so much light on the realities faced by women throughout the 1900s.

ISBN 9781925581287

Adoption Deception
Penny Mackieson

What is it like to be adopted, have your identity changed and never feel quite at home in your new family, despite being loved? What is it like to become a social worker and be faced with the challenges and consequences of other adoptions every day? Penny Mackieson takes us on her journey with the unique perspective of both the adopted person and a professional working in the field, and presents a compelling argument for policy change.

ISBN 9781742199740

Dark Matters: A novel
Susan Hawthorne

When Desi inherits her aunt Kate's house she begins to read the contents of the boxes in the back room. Among the papers are records of arrest, imprisonment and torture at the hands of an unknown group who persecute her for her sexuality and activism. Scraps of memoir, family history and poems complete this fragmented story as Desi uncovers Kate's hidden life. Can Desi find Kate's lover, Mercedes, who had escaped from Pinochet's Chile? Where is she and can she help unravel Kate's story?

ISBN 9781925581089

Bite Your Tongue
Francesca Rendle-Short

This is the story of a teenage girl growing up in conservative Queensland during the 1970s, a time of great social upheaval. Her mother is Angel/Mother Joy, a morals crusader, whose fervor against change includes a list of books to ban and burn. This is also the story of the daughter as an adult and a writer, facing her mother's mortality while at the same time 'discovering' her in archival materials. A unique mix of novel and memoir in captivating storytelling that brings to life the clash of family and politics with humour and tenderness.

ISBN 9781876756963

Dark Matter: New Poems
Robin Morgan

In this major new book of poems, her seventh, Robin Morgan rewards us with the award-winning mastery we've come to expect from her poetry. Her gaze is unflinching, her craft sharp, her mature voice rich with wry wit, survived pain, and her signature chord: an indomitable celebration of life.

ISBN 9781925581430

Goja
Suniti Namjoshi

Growing up a princess in the ruling house of Maharashtra, the two most important relationships in the author's life were with her grandmother Goldie and with Goja, the servant woman who slept beside her bed. In beautifully crafted prose, Suniti Namjoshi converses in her head with the two women, talking about the clash of cultures of East and West, class privilege and poverty, language and literacy, shedding light on the multiple contradictions in her life.

ISBN 9781875559978

*If you would like to know more about
Spinifex Press, write to us for a free catalogue, visit our
website or email us for further information
on how to subscribe to our monthly newsletter.*

Spinifex Press
PO Box 105
Mission Beach QLD 4852
Australia

www.spinifexpress.com.au
women@spinifexpress.com.au